The Great GALLOON and the PIRATE QUEEN

The Great Galloon and the Pirate Queen

Being a continuation, and perhaps even
a conclusion of sorts, to the tale of
Captain Meredith Anstruther, his fantastical
vessel and crew, and their efforts to defeat
the most dastardly of foes.

Tom Banks

HOT
KEY
BOOKS

First published in Great Britain in 2015 by Hot Key Books
Northburgh House, 10 Northburgh Street, London EC1V 0AT

A CIP catalogue record for this book is available from the British Library.

ISBN: 978-1-8481-2450-9

1

Typeset by Palimpsest Book Production Limited, Falkirk, Stirlingshire
This book is set in 11.75 pt Sabon LT Std

Printed and bound by Clays Ltd, St Ives Plc

FSC

Hot Key Books supports the Forest Stewardship Council (FSC), the leading
international forest certification organisation, and is committed to printing
only on Greenpeace-approved FSC-certified paper.

www.hotkeybooks.com

Hot Key Books is part of the Bonnier Publishing Group
www.bonnierpublishing.com

No Slugs We

Dear Reader,

Throughout these stories of 'The Great Galloon' you will find 'Goodnight points'. You may or may not be familiar with these. If not, why haven't you read the other stories about the Galloon? You should. Not now! Read this one. But after you've finished, beg, borrow or buy the others. 'Goodnight points' provide you, or whoever is reading this to you, an opportunity to put the book down and tell you to go to sleep. After whoever it is has gone, you should pick the book back up again and look for the bit where one of the characters says 'Bumcheek'.

Chapter One

In which the author realises that this book
doesn't have chapters, so it's all chapter one.

Stanley watched in awe as Captain Meredith Anstruther leapt around the wheelhouse of his fabled Great Galloon, yanking levers, tapping dials, and wrestling with the mighty brassbound wheel. Outside, the wind was howling, the rain was lashing down, and the clouds loomed all around like disapproving relatives. The Galloon had run straight into a storm, and it was everything the crew could do to keep her steady.

'Give number twelve a tweak, Stanley!' boomed the Captain, his being perhaps the only voice in the world that could compete with the screaming of the storm.

'Aye aye, Cap'n!' said Stanley. He threw both arms

round one of the tall wooden levers that was sticking out of the floor, and pulled on it for all he was worth. It creaked and strained, and moved about an inch towards him.

'Woah!' cried the Captain. 'That's it! That's it, lad! And now read off that dial!'

Stanley looked to where the Captain was pointing at what he had assumed was a clock. As the Galloon pitched and rolled, he squinted at the two long black hands on it.

'Erm – the long hand's pointing to "Mustn't Grumble" and the short hand's pointing to "Turned out nice again",' he shouted.

'That can't be right, begad!' boomed the Captain. With one hand on the wheel, he reached across the wheelhouse and tapped the dial with a huge finger. The hands began to spin, and Stanley watched as they came to rest again.

'Now they're both pointing at "Nice weather for ducks"!' cried Stanley.

'Well, that's something, eh?' said the Captain.

Stanley nodded and laughed, though he didn't know what something it was. The Galloon pitched again, and Stanley was thrown against the plate-glass window. Through it he could see the rain, hammering down on the for'ard deck of the Great Galloon, and little else. They were in the middle of a storm such as Stanley had never seen before. Every plank and rope on the Great Galloon was straining to its limit. Lightning flashed, and Stanley saw the great vessel outlined sharply for a second. The deck stretched out before him, rising to the enormous prow, all overtopped by the tangle of sails and balloons that kept them moving through the sky. As the lightning crackled, a shape hurtled by. Stanley saw long black wings, and a yellow beak, before the darkness reclaimed them.

'Fishbane!' shouted Stanley, but the shape was gone. Stanley thought he heard the sound of a cry on the wind:

'KRAAAAWWW-KAK-KAK-KAK-KAK-KAK-KAK-
SKWEEEEEEEEEEEE-KRAAAAAAAWWWWW!'

But could see no more. The Captain however, was listening hard.

'The observatory, you say, my wingéd friend?' he said. 'Very well!'

With his dark eyes flashing in the strange, green light of the storm, the Captain spun round, grabbed Stanley around the waist with one great arm, and flung open the door of the wheelhouse.

'Woooo-hooooo!' yelled Stanley.

The wind was now absurdly loud. It blew in through the door and set the levers and pulleys rattling. Stanley was grateful for the Captain's vicelike grip around his waist. The Captain was looking at a bank of small white plungers, like door knobs or organ stops, set in the back wall of the wheelhouse. He selected one that had 'Ducks, nice weather for . . .' written on it, and one that said 'Why not try this one?' Then he hesitated, before pulling another that said 'Storm in a teacup' on it. This done, he turned towards the door, and with one hand on the doorframe, managed to heave himself and Stanley out of the wheelhouse and into the maelstrom. As they stepped out, Stanley felt the rain slapping against his face like a shower of angry sprats. It made him gasp, which only made him cough and splutter. It was as close to being underwater as it was possible to be while actually being a few hundred feet up in the air. The Captain took a moment to steady himself, and then began to make his way, ever so carefully, across the deck.

'---- ----- ---!' cried Stanley, his words whipped away almost before he could think them.

'-- ----- ---!' agreed the Captain.

I wish Rasmussen were here, so we could talk to each other in sign language, thought Stanley to himself.

Just at that moment, as the Captain clung to the quarterdeck rail, and Stanley clung onto the Captain, another sound joined the howling of the wind and the crashing of the thunder. Through the grey sheet of rain, Stanley saw a shape come into view through the clouds alongside the Galloon. It was a spindly, wiry contraption, with huge spinning rotors, like a windmill's skeleton. Its long thin rotor blades were cracking like whips as they chopped up the air. It wobbled crazily, and jinked to avoid a packing crate that had been blown from the deck. Then it dipped and went out of sight, before slowly reappearing slightly closer. The rain obscured Stanley's view for a moment, but he felt the Captain laugh, and then gasp. Through a flurry of rain, Stanley saw it was the gyrocopter, one of the many flying contraptions that followed the Great Galloon.

Through its windshield Stanley could see two figures. One was a woman in a leather hat, who seemed to be struggling with the controls. Beside her, and closer to Stanley, was a smaller figure, in a green dressing gown, with its feet on the dashboard, and a sandwich in its hands.

'Rasmussen!' he shouted.

Rasmussen, Stanley's infuriating best friend, looked up, as if she were sitting in a sunlounger on a deserted beach, and gave Stanley a little wave. In the private sign language she and Stanley had created for just such occasions as this, she said, 'You look like a drowned kipper,' and went back to her sandwich.

Beside her, her mother, the Countess of Hammerstein, looked across and smiled. She tried to mouth something at Stanley and the Captain –

'"We've clotted the bland macaroon"?' said Stanley.

'No, no, she's saying . . .' The Captain squinted through his eyeglass . . . '"We've knotted the random buffoon". Can that be right?'

'I can't see properly, their windows are steamed up!' called Stanley.

Rasmussen yanked the window back with both hands. Her sandwich, which she had been holding in her mouth, was immediately whipped away by the wind. She glared at Stanley with a force that rivalled the storm itself, and signed with both hands, in the language that she and Stanley had created for eventualities such as this.

'WE.'

'We,' said Stanley, now looking through the eyeglass that the Captain had lent him.

'HAVE.'

'Have.'

'SPOTTED.'

'Could be "spotted", "splatted" or "twinkly".'

'THE.'

'Wednesday. No! The.'

'GRAND.'

'Grand – or stinky. Her finger actions are very imprecise.'

'SUMBAROON.'

'Either "racehorse" or "Sumbaroon".'

Stanley turned to see the Captain scribbling the words down in a soggy notebook. Looking back he saw the gyrocopter pitch wildly as another piece of debris tumbled by, then, as it came back into view, he saw Rasmussen frantically throwing shapes with her hands.

'She seems cross!' said the Captain. 'What's she saying now?'

'She's saying we owe her a jam and herring sandwich,' said Stanley, giving back the telescope, and making the sign for 'fair enough'.

'Fair enough,' said the Captain.

The Countess pointed frantically down towards the sea, and then the gyrocopter waggled a goodbye, before banking away to relative safety.

'So what's the message again?' said Stanley.

'Errm, let me see. It says, "We have splatted the stinky racehorse". Or "We have spotted the Grand Sumbaroon".'

The look on the Captain's face told Stanley everything. 'That poor racehorse!' he said, and felt a lump in his throat.

'Erm, I think perhaps, it's the second one,' said the Captain, patiently.

'Right! Of course. Silly me. So they've spotted the Grand Sumbaroon.'

The impact of this took a moment to make its way through Stanley's embarrassment. When he did, his head snapped up and he and the Captain beamed at each other.

'They've spotted the Grand Sumbaroon!' they shouted, together.

GOODNIGHT!

The chase was on. If Stanley thought the Captain had been impressive before, he was positively awe inspiring now.

It was later that day – the Captain had still not slept or eaten. Indeed he had barely even spoken, except to bark out orders. He was running from one part of the quarterdeck to another, testing lines, staring into the storm, taking readings from a wide variety of instruments.

'Hard a-port and lower the outriggers!' he cried at one point.

'Tighten your slack there, Mr Tump, and we'll make another four knots!' at another.

The Galloon, despite her massive size, was fairly racing along in the storm, her lines humming and her mainsail taut as a drum skin. Stanley tripped over a stack of hammocks as he tried to keep up with the Captain.

'Careful, lad! You're no use to me with a broken ankle!' said the great man, and Stanley felt a thrill at the idea of being useful at all, broken ankle or no. He staggered to his feet, and saw the Captain disappear into the driving rain, bellowing as he went.

Stanley upped and followed, and was just in time to see him crouch down near the boatswain's chair. He was pleased to see the Captain beckon him over. In the relative shelter of the rail, talking was easier.

'To the observatory, lad,' said the Captain. 'What's the quickest way, d'you think?'

'Err – take the lift down to the 'tween deck, then along to the grand staircase, slide down the bannister, through the false back of the broom cupboard, into the dumb waiter, and down?' said Stanley, sticking his tongue out with the effort of remembering.

'That's a way, yes, and a fine way when you're not with me,' said the Captain. He stopped, turned, and held Stanley by the shoulders. 'Or we could walk the plank!'

'We could walk the what now?' said Stanley, a huge smile spreading over his face.

'You heard me, Stanley. Are you game?'

'Yes, sir!'

'For the last time, I'm no more a sir than you are a goblin!' The Captain looked Stanley over briefly, from the crumpled unicorn's horn on his head to the ends of his blue furry fingers. 'You're not a goblin, are you?'

'Shouldn't think so. What's a goblin?' said Stanley, still smiling.

'Well – quite.' This seemed to be enough for the Captain, who snapped to attention again. 'The plank, I say! Let's go.'

They moved quickly towards the pointy front end of the ship, and were soon standing by a capstan, a thick iron post with a rope wrapped round it. The Captain immediately put his back to the handle that made the capstan turn, and the rope began to unwind. Stanley tried to help, but could barely reach, so he ended up standing on top of the iron contraption, peeping over the edge of the Galloon, where a gap in the rail meant he could see down to the clouds below.

'What's it doing!?' he yelled.

'Watch, boy!' yelled the Captain. 'You'll see!'

Stanley looked out again, and this time he caught a glimpse of something – as the Captain pushed, a plank was beginning to emerge from the deck of the Galloon, and heave itself out over the void.

'Tarheel!' bellowed the Captain, his enormous voice carrying through the storm. 'To me, my friend!'

Crewman Tarheel, struggling by with a coil of rope in his hand, joined the Captain at the capstan, and soon Stanley was watching the plank extending from the deck of the Galloon like a ruler on an almighty desk. It thrummed in a similar way, as the wind caught it, and Stanley couldn't quite believe that the Captain was planning to walk out on the plank – and to what end?

He didn't know, but he had learned a long time ago to trust the Captain in even his strangest decisions.

'Thank 'ee, Tarheel!' cried the Captain, and as the crewman saluted, he waved a hand dismissively.

'Wish I could stop people doing that!' he said to Stanley. 'Maybe, Stanley, when you're the . . . never mind. The plank is out – let's walk it.'

Stanley clambered down from the capstan, and grabbed onto the rail for safety. He watched as the Captain lay down on his front, and edged his way to the very lip of the deck – below him, the swirling storm, and the raging sea. Stanley's heart was thumping in his throat, not for the first time in his adventures with the Captain. But he followed. Lying down on the deck, he half crawled, half shuffled out onto the oaken plank that served as a gangway when they were in port, but now felt worryingly like a diving board. The Captain was now a person's length away from the deck, and Stanley was right behind him. Stanley told himself that if the Captain was doing it, it must be okay – though he could hear the voice of his friend the Countess telling him that the Captain was only a man, and a man who made as many mistakes as anyone else.

From this angle, he could see mainly the soles of the Captain's enormous boots, inches from his head. The Captain called something over his shoulder, but the noise of the storm was so intense here that Stanley could not make it out. The Captain was pointing down and out – so that's where Stanley looked.

The gyrocopter was now chuntering along below them. As he stared through the cloud and rain, Stanley could see the side of the Galloon dropping away into the far distance. And next to it, only a few feet clear, the gyrocopter seemed to be keeping pace with them. The Galloon was still racing along, its steam-powered automatic pilot system keeping them on course, so Stanley knew that the gyrocopter was probably flying flat out to keep up. As he watched, the clattering machine began to rise towards them, until it was hovering about twenty feet from the end of the plank.

'Corks,' said Stanley aloud. 'He's not going to . . . ?'

'I am, lad!' yelled the Captain. 'And so are you! No time for the long way round – this is how we get to the observatory before the Sumbaroon dives and loses us forever!'

A gust caught the plank, and for a moment Stanley thought all was lost. But the Captain seemed to be the sturdiest thing in this wind-whipped world. He carefully lifted himself to a standing position. Stanley couldn't believe his eyes. Hurtling through the skies, in a storm that registered 'Cor blimey' on the Rasmussen scale, the Captain stood calmly on the plank as if it were a bowling green. He held out his enormous hands for Stanley, who grabbed them tightly and tried his best to stand up.

'On my boots, lad – you'll be steadier there!' said the Captain.

Stanley stepped up onto the Captain's boat-like boots. He was soaked to the skin, terrified for his life, and happier than he could ever remember being. The gyrocopter thumped the air below them.

'Where is the observatory, Stanley?' cried the Captain.

'On the keel, sir, down below. Lowest point of the Galloon.'

'Yes indeedy – and when you're up high, and you need to be low, the quickest way is . . . ?'

'To . . . fall?' said Stanley above the howling.

'Yup!' said the Captain – and together, they fell.

Stanley's words, breath and fear were stolen away by the wind. Then the Captain was reaching out with one enormous hand, holding both of Stanley's in the other. He grabbed something – Stanley's eyes were now shut tight, but he assumed it was part of the gyrocopter – and then they weren't falling any more, but flying. The 'copter veered away, and started taking them down, down towards the sea. They were pulling away, flying in a wide arc underneath the great vessel. With streaming eyes, Stanley searched for their target – a tiny bubble of glass on the keel of the Galloon, known as the observatory. It was like looking for a drawing pin on a football field.

They were now right underneath the great flying ship, and coming up again. From here he could see the invisibarnacles, skyweed and crab-rot that clung to the bottom. The observatory itself was now visible – a kind of domed window just sturdy enough for two people to clamber inside. The gyrocopter, though expertly flown by the Countess, was in real peril of being smashed against the keel. As they approached the glass dome, the Captain let go of one of Stanley's hands.

'The catch, lad!' he bellowed.

Stanley looked, and saw that the dome was closed with a simple latch.

'Home and dry!' the Captain shouted, and he smiled. Stanley reached out, and easily flicked open the window. There was a slight lurch from the 'copter, but soon he was back in place, and he grabbed the windowsill.

'After you!' cried the Captain.

Stanley carefully leapt from the Captain's boots, so now he was hanging by both hands from the bottom-most point of the Galloon. The gyrocopter was rock steady, and as Stanley pulled himself inside, the Captain also made the leap. Stanley was now inside the dome, face down on the glass, while the Captain squeezed in behind him. The noise was still phenomenal, but once they were both inside the observatory, the Captain turned to him and spoke in a more normal voice.

'I think we can close that now!'

As the gyrocopter pulled away, Stanley reached out

and grabbed the latch of the open window. The view below him was truly astounding – they were low over the sea, and the crests of the waves were like white horses galloping along. He stopped to look for a moment, and then yanked the window shut. Stanley breathed out, but there was no time to relax.

'Look, Stanley!' said the Captain, pointing down at the sea. 'Look what we would have landed on if we'd fallen!'

There, only a few dozen feet below them now they were at the lowest point of the Great Galloon, was a great grey shape, shoving its way through the sea. It bashed and crashed into every wave, but seemed to be making good progress nonetheless – it was slowly pulling away from them.

'The Grand Sumbaroon!' murmured Captain Anstruther.

'And on it, your despicable brother, who made off with your wife-to-be, Isabella, just moments before you were due to marry her!' said Stanley.

The Captain gave him a funny look.

'Yes, thank you, Stanley, I know all that. I have thought of little else since that fateful day. But the end is in sight – I will not lose them again. Even in this storm.'

'But the Sumbaroon can dive, can't it? And get away unseen?'

'It is my belief that the Sumbaroon will struggle to dive for long in this swell – even at the best of times it cannot stay below for longer than an hour or two. As long as we keep track of its course, we should be able to follow it wherever it goes. We will rescue my Isabella soon.'

'Well – that's good. And then we can have some wedding cake at last,' said Stanley.

GOODNIGHT!

Cloudier Peele was whooping. She didn't often allow herself a good whoop, as she did not see herself as the whooping type. Whooping, she felt, was for jolly people in multicoloured clothes. People who might say things like 'chin up', and 'You have to laugh!?' But whoop she did, and here's why.

She was standing in the crow's nest high up the mainmast of the phenomenally huge flying ship, with lightning crackling all around her, the rain in her face, and the rush of the wind in her hair. The main balloon itself loomed over her like a storm cloud made of dark red canvas. Usually this was enough to keep the worst

17

of the wind and rain away, but today the water was being whipped from the sea below and the clouds above. It was being thrown about by the wind in such a way that there was no dry corner to be found. Her velvet dress was ruined, her book of interesting thoughts was now a mush of soggy pages, but she had given in to exhilaration, and it felt great. She even did a little dance, because no-one was watching.

She had been here quite a lot recently, spending time with her friend who was a boy, Clamdigger. He too was away right now, but the fact that he might pop up through the lubbers' hole at any moment, was at least part of what made Cloudier dance.

As she so often did, she felt a sudden rush of self-consciousness, and sat down heavily on the little bench that ran round the inside of the crow's nest. She put an eye to the powerful telescope that stood nearby, and peered out. Although she was many feet above the deck, her field of view was limited by the gigantic balloon above, the ship itself below, and the rigging and sails that surrounded her. But she could see the horizon all around, and she peered at it intently. She knew that many members of the Galloon's crew were out there in the storm, hoping to spot the Grand Sumbaroon, and give chase. She secretly hoped to be the first to see it.

A small brassbound box on the bench beside her hissed and spat, drawing her away from the search.

'The Squeaking Tube!' she cried, dramatically, and leaned down to listen, a hand cupped round one ear.

A tiny voice began to speak from the box. With the cracking and hissing that came with it, and the noise of the storm all around, Cloudier could make out only a few words, but they were enough.

'. . . sssssss . . . kkkk . . . all hands, attention all hands . . . well, ears, I suppose . . . ffffffttttfffft Captain speaking from the observatory . . . have spotted my dastardly brother . . . heading west nor'west by starboard, forty degrees at twelve o'clock, occasionally poor, growing fine later . . . Ms Huntley, you have the bridge . . . kkttthhffffffsst . . . turn this damn thing off . . .'

The wind in Cloudier's face blew even harder as the Galloon picked up speed. She knew that, down in the bowels of the great vessel, the Brunt would be shovelling coal into the furnace, to give the Galloon as much power as possible. The lines around Cloudier hummed and whistled as the Galloon raced along. She looked through the telescope again, and saw that many of the flying craft that had been searching the seas were now in formation, gathered around the prow of the enormous ship. Although they were hundreds of metres away, with the telescope she could see the gyrocopter flitting around, the Seagle Fishbane diving and swooping, She could just make out the stripy jumper of Clamdigger, who was piloting the old steam-powered airbus known as the charabanc, and for a moment she allowed herself a daydream of sitting next to him, and tootling off into the wide blue yonder. But she found even the daydream embarrassing, and snapped back to reality as the charabanc dived out of sight. She grabbed the Squeaking Tube and spoke into it as clearly as possible.

'Cloudier to Captain, over. Can you give me an update on the status of Mr Clamdigger, over. I've lost visual contact, over.'

'Erm, Cloudier,' said a small voice that wasn't the Captain's. 'You don't say "over" 'til you've finished what you want to say. Over.'

Cloudier knew this was Stanley. She waited to see if he was going to say anything else.

'That is, you only say "over" when you're not going to say anything else. Over.'

'Oh, right,' she said. 'I thought it was just the thing you said when talking into a contraption like this.'

Silence.

'Over,' she added.

'No – it just means it's the other person's turn to talk. Over,' said Stanley.

'I see. So it's a way of making sure we don't talk over . . .'

'Yes,' said Stanley.

'. . . each other. Over,' she finished.

21

'Erm. Yes,' said Stanley, his voice sounding like a little lost mouse once it had negotiated the miles and miles of tubing that now snaked its way all around the Galloon. Clamdigger had realised, during the affair of the Kraken's Lair, that a way of communicating all around the ship would be very useful, and so he had spent every spare minute since installing this network of pipes, which had quickly become known as the 'Squeaking Tubes'. It was indeed very useful, but it was taking some getting used to.

'Is the Captain there? Can you see Clamdigger, over?' she said.

'The Captain's gone back to the wheelhouse to help Ms Huntley,' said Stanley. 'But between you and me we should be able to see most of the outflyers. Yes – I can see Clamdigger. My, he's really flying that old bus! He's being thrown around a bit but it looks like he's trying to bring it low over the Sumbaroon. Yes, he's aiming straight for it, but the wind is trying to throw him off course! He's wrestling with the controls . . .'

'Go on, Clamdigger!' shouted Cloudier, unable to stop herself. Then, realising she was in danger of losing her cool: 'Or don't, you know. Whevs.'

But she held the Squeaking Tube to her ear nonetheless as Stanley's commentary continued.

'The Sumbaroon – it's dipped below the surface – and now . . . and now . . .'

'Now whaaaat?!' squealed Cloudier.

'The Sumbaroon is leaping like a dolphin! And again! It seems to be surfing along on the crests of the waves, and then leaping high, and falling back into the sea! Clamdigger seems determined to stay with it! But . . . it's leaping again! It's jumped right over . . . !'

'You can't stop there!' screamed Cloudier, entirely forgetting to be insouciant, nonchalant, or any of those other things she would never admit to being.

'No! This isn't that kind of "over", this is just me saying "It's leapt right *over* him!" He's been doused with spray! He's wobbling! The Sumbaroon has gone – it's dived out of sight! I think the charabanc has water in its engines! It's spluttering! He's clipped a wave!'

'Come on, Jack Clamdigger!' hissed Cloudier.

'He's ditched! He's in the sea!' cried Stanley. 'The Sumbaroon is diving out of sight!'

Cloudier literally put her fist in her mouth as she listened in.

'Stanley to wheelhouse! Ms Huntley! Clamdigger's in the sea, and he's in danger! It's too rough for the 'copter too! We'll have to stop and rescue him! Stanley to wheelhouse, do you read me? Over.'

'All hands, full stop, please!' came Ms Huntley's voice.

As soon as Ms Huntley had said the words, Cloudier

23

heard movement in the rigging, and a great bell began to clang. The shout of 'Full stop!' rang out around the Galloon, and she immediately felt the loss of speed. In fact, it came close to tipping her out of the crow's nest. She grabbed the Squeaking Tube to steady herself, and heard the Captain's voice, slightly out of breath.

'What the . . . ?' he boomed. 'The Sumbaroon! Ms Huntley, the Sumbaroon must not get away!'

'No, Captain,' said her mother's voice, gentler but no less firm. 'Clamdigger is in danger. We must save him. I have called for a full stop.'

The Galloon bucked like a mule, albeit a mule the size of a market town, and came to a stop. The wind still howled, the rain still battered Cloudier from all sides, but they were no longer racing before the storm.

The Captain, too, seemed to have become calmer.

'Yes, Harissa,' he said using Ms Huntley's first name. 'You are right as always. Ask Mr Abel to make the chairlift ready – I will see to Mr Clamdigger myself, and only then will we continue the search for the Grand Sumbaroon.'

'Aye aye, Captain,' said Ms Huntley. 'And Cloudier – you can stop listening now.'

'Yes, Mum!' said Cloudier, taken by surprise. 'I mean, aye aye, Ms Huntley!'

She put the Squeaking Tube back into its holder. If Clamdigger was going to be rescued, she was going to

make sure she just happened to be coincidentally nearby
when he came back onboard.

GOODNIGHT!

Three days later, the Galloon was in the Dumps. Not
just figuratively – though there was a certain pall over
everything, since they had lost sight of the Sumbaroon
– but also literally. The Dumps was an area in the Wide
Blue Ocean where the winds did not blow. The storm
that had brought them here had died down as suddenly
as it had begun. By the time Clamdigger had been
plucked from the hull of the charabanc, which sadly
sunk without trace soon after, the Galloon was drifting
around in a dull grey sky. Its sails were hung out to
dry, and crewmembers were clambering all over the
deck, flogging the water off with rags and towels. Even
the main balloon itself was undergoing some much-
needed repair, with teams of harnessed Gallooniers
scouring it for rips and tears.

Stanley and Rasmussen did not get involved in this
stuff, of course – although they were always willing to
help out in a crisis, they did not like to get too distracted

from their main business, which was seeking adventure. Stanley had wanted to start a club called the Adventure-Seekers, but Rasmussen had said that was unnecessarily exclusive, and that they should just remain a loose collective of adventure seekers. So that's what they were. Over the years they had been friends, they had come close to adventure a few times – Stanley had once seen a flying object that he could not identify, but Rasmussen had soon revealed it simply to be a UFO. Rasmussen once thought she'd found a 'secret door' map, but owing to a spelling error it had turned out to be a 'secret doormat', which wasn't nearly as exciting. They had wiped their feet on it anyway, but there the adventure had ended. Other than that, they had spent most of their time together just battling monster moths, discovering robot stowaways, and abseiling through a snowstorm onto a live volcano. Rasmussen for one was getting sick of it.

'All I ask for is an adventure!' she moaned.

'There was that time you fell off the Galloon, and the Captain had to rescue you with a boat hook,' said Stanley.

'Yes, while people were firing cannonballs at us,' said Rasmussen, 'but I mean proper adventure, with derring-do, and ne'er-do-wells all over the place!'

'What are those things?' asked Stanley.

'I don't know!' shouted Rasmussen. 'I've never met

26

a derring-do, or been involved in a ne'er-do-well of any sort!'

'Well, we'll just have to keep an eye out,' said Stanley.

They were sitting in Stanley's little room, on a lower deck of the Galloon. They had pushed the furniture to the sides of the room, and copied out a map of the Wide Blue Ocean in chalk on the floorboards. They were trying to work out where the Grand Sumbaroon of Zebediah Anstruther would have got to by now. The Captain himself had gone into full cursing and glowering mode, stomping around the Galloon, calling meetings with Ms Huntley, Skyman Abel and the other senior people onboard, but barely speaking to anyone else. He could be seen once a day sweeping into the mess to grab a lunch tray, but then he would storm off to his cabin to eat in peace.

'Look,' said Rasmussen, idly swinging her foot towards the spot on their impromptu map marked 'The Dumps'. 'We lost him here, right?'

'Yeeees,' said Stanley, rolling his eyes at the idea of Rasmussen going through all this for the nine hundredth time that morning.

'And he was heading this way, right? Towards Longnight Island?'

'You know he was,' said Stanley, pouring himself another cup of tea.

'But he was underwater, and by the time the storm

had lifted, we couldn't see him. Even Fishbane had lost the trail.'

'Yes – but the Grand Sumbaroon is still damaged from its run-in with the great whale. It can't stay below for more than an hour. If he'd doubled back, we would have seen him. So, as the Captain has people in every harbour on Havnabruck, and there's nowhere to the south for Zebediah to go, he must be at Long-night. But we can't follow him, because we're stuck in the Dumps, with no wind. We just have to wait.' Stanley slurped his tea, and picked a book off the shelf.

'Who says he can't go south?' said Rasmussen, scratching a mark through the chalk with her mother's cane.

'Have you never paid attention in a Geography lesson!?' said Stanley.

'I've never been to a Geography lesson. But look at the map.'

Stanley looked at it. Especially at the new scratch that Rasmussen had made. A deep, long scratch through the green of the Baroco rainforest, to the south of the ocean.

'I'm looking, said Stanley. 'And all I can see is the impregnable forest and enormous cliffs along the whole of the Baroco coast. All the way down to . . . to . . .'

'To the Great Brown Greasy Rococo River,' said

Rasmussen, pointing to where her newly scratched river met the sea on the map.

'But . . . the Sumbaroon couldn't swim up a river, could it?' said Stanley. And even if it could, why would it? We'd have it cornered, there'd be nowhere for it to go except deeper into the forest. What would be the point of that? What could they possibly find there?'

'I can only think of one thing that you can find in the heart of the darkest forest, with ancient trees and mysterious civilisations all around,' said Rasmussen, staring at the map.

Stanley stared at it too. He slurped his tea.

'Yup,' he said.

Rasmussen ground her teeth.

'Ask me then,' she said.

'But I know,' said Stanley.

'Just ask me!' hissed Rasmussen.

'Okay!' said Stanley. 'What's the only thing you can find in the heart of the darkest forest, with ancient trees and mysterious civilisations all around?'

'Adventure!' said Rasmussen, with a grin.

'Oh right!' said Stanley with a smile. 'I was thinking "creepy crawlies". But adventure is much better. Well done.'

As they stood up to leave, a crackling noise made Stanley stop in his tracks.

'The Examinator!' he said.

'No time!' said Rasmussen. 'We've got to tell the Captain that we've worked out where the Sumbaroon is going.'

'But we don't know . . . we just suspect. We don't even know if the Sumbaroon can go up a river! Anyway, why is the Examinator crackling? It's not lesson time.'

The Examinator was a large box on a desk in Stanley's room. It had two aerials poking out of the top, and a glass valve on the side that got hot. In front was a shell-shaped object with 'Speak Here' written on it. Stanley used it to communicate with his parents, who were also its inventors. They were back in his home village of Mirrorwater. His mother was a teacher, so he also had lessons over the Examinator every day. But it had never spontaneously crackled into life before. At least, not when he'd been in the room. A light flashed, and a needle in a little dial moved from 'Nobody There' to 'Who's This?'.

A voice spoke from the little mesh on the front of the contraption.

'This is Big Dipper, come in? Big Dipper to anyone out there, come in?'

'How can we come in? We are in!' said Rasmussen sharply.

'Shh!' said Stanley. 'She can't hear you. Who's Big Dipper anyway? Silly name.'

'Why Big Dipper?' said a girl's voice from the speaker. 'Silly name.'

'There's a boy and a girl,' said Rasmussen. 'She sounds very cross.'

'Big Dipper!' said the boy on the Examinator. 'Because we're big and we dip under the water! We can't very well go around saying "Grand Sumbaroon", can we? What would Captain Zebediah say?'

Stanley and Rasmussen's jaws hit the floor. Literally, as they both fell over with the shock.

'Who cares what he says?' said the Examinator girl. 'I'm even beginning to think he might not be quite the hero he pretends to be . . .'

'Shhh!' said the boy. 'That's mutiny! Anyway, there's no-one out there to hear us. Probably for the best, as we won't be able to get much reception once we're swimming up the Great Brown Greasy Rococo River anyway. This is Big Dipper, signing out. 10-40 big buddy.'

'What does "10-40 big buddy" mean? Is it code?' said the girl.

'No,' said the boy. 'It's the time. Nearly elevenses. Let's go . . .'

And the Examinator crackled again, and went silent. Stanley ran to it, and began to fiddle with knobs and twiddle buttons, while Rasmussen hopped from leg to leg behind him, singing the 'we just found out where the Sumbaroon is' song she had written for just this moment.

31

'Nobody there!' said Stanley after a few frantic moments.

'We've got to tell the Captain!' they shouted together. And stopping only to grab a biscuit, as they'd been reminded it was practically elevenses, they went to do just that.

GOODNIGHT!

Cloudier was back in the crow's nest. With the Galloon hanging stationary in the sky like a bad mood, her cosy little weather balloon would not stay aloft for long without using up a lot of fuel, so she had decamped up here again to do her lookout duty. Clamdigger, who normally occupied the little wooden basket on the mainmast, was busy organising the towing party. With the Galloon completely becalmed, and not much to look out for, she had time for her favourite pastimes – reading, and feeling sorry for herself.

She only had her notebook up here, not the little personal library she carried with her in the weather balloon, and while coming through the storms had been pretty terrifying, it had kept her busy. She had tried writing poetry, as was her passion. That had not turned out as she'd hoped. Having noticed a certain unintended *theme* developing in her work, she had made a pledge not to write about anything that could be thought of as being to do with boys. One boy in particular. And so she had tried to write a poem about the sunset.

Like a great clam, in its stripy-jumpered shell,
The sun sets below the sea's swell.
Nothing in my world seems bigger.
The day will dig it out, like a cla—

At this point she had slammed the book closed, and begun scribbling on the cover. Now the only thing to keep her occupied was the rattling and juddering that told her someone big was climbing up the mainmast towards her.

Ooo! Someone was coming. She dropped her book and leaned over to look through the lubber's hole.

Strange, she thought, *could have sworn I heard someone.*

'Cloudier Peele, as I live and breathe!' said a booming voice behind her. She nearly leapt out of her skin, and spun round to see the Captain clambering over the outside rail of the crow's nest.

'Looking down the lubber's hole for me! Ha! You

33

won't find me using that. It's for landspeople and cowards! I come round the outside or not at all.'

He landed squarely on the boards of the crow's nest with a thump. Cloudier was pleased to see that, despite his gloom since losing the Sumbaroon, he had a glint in his eye. He always did when he was out and about on his beloved Galloon.

'Oh,' she said, 'I come through the hole, I'm afraid.'

'And so you should. Load of showy nonsense, this "round the outside" stuff. Could get meself killed, and then where would we be?'

Cloudier didn't know what to say.

'Well, you'd be here, clearly. But you'd no doubt be a bit miffed with having to deal with it, and I . . . would . . . be dead,' said the Captain.

'What a lot of piffle,' he continued. 'Sorry, Miss Peele, I've been locked inside my own head for a day or so, sometimes it's hard to come out. How's things up here? Spotted anything?'

'No, Captain. Just the sea. Smooth as glass all around. There's a cloud over there, but it's not done much. No sign of your . . . of the Sumbaroon, I'm afraid.'

'I'm afraid too – that's why I had to get out for a wander. But of course it's hard to see far from here. The weather balloon gives a better view. Or we could go up to the top, of course.'

Cloudier thought for a moment. She pictured the

Galloon in her mind, and where they were, near the top of the mainmast, with the vast bulk of the mainb'loon hanging over their heads.

'To the top? Are we not at the top?'

'Wha? Bless my clichéd barnacles, no, we are not at the top. Have you not wondered where that goes? You young people – too much respect for your elders, not nearly enough poking around in corners, asking awkward questions and so on.'

As he spoke, the Captain put his hands to the great mizzenmast, which was made of twelve stout trees lashed in a bundle. Cloudier noticed for the first time that hammered into the mast were iron pegs, like footholds. She looked up, and saw that 'where that goes' referred to the point where the mast actually entered the mainb'loon itself. The Captain was climbing now, and as so often before, Cloudier wasn't sure if he expected her to follow or not.

'I thought it just kind of stopped!' she said.

'Thought? What's the point in thinking when you could be looking? Come on. You've spent enough time in the crow's nest – let's show you the eagle's lair.'

Cloudier, astonished that there was yet more of the Galloon to see, began to climb after the Captain in a determined manner.

After they'd climbed up a few more feet, the Captain stopped, just below where the mast entered the balloon.

He began pulling at the edge of the balloon where it met the mast. Eventually he yanked it over his head like he was getting into a sleeping bag the wrong way round. Then he heaved himself up another step or two, and was gone. The edge of the balloon, with some kind of rubber seal round it, snapped back against the mast, and before long looked exactly as it had done before.

Cloudier stared, and was soon aware that something more was required. So she pulled up the hem of her black dress, which she had taken care to make a good six inches too long so that it got wet and muddy as it dragged along the ground, thereby proving that she didn't care about it. She flung it over one arm, and feeling like Rambleschnitzel the fairytale goblin, who lived in a spinning wheel and wove her magical hair into golden hay because she couldn't remember her name (or something), she began to climb.

If he can just go in there, I can too . . . she thought to herself, but knew full well that where the Galloon was concerned, there were many things that the Captain could do that others would struggle with. This was not a comforting thing to be thinking as she put a hand to the warm red canvas of the mainb'loon, and pulled at the seam where it met the mast. A gust of warm air, like the breath of a friendly rubber cow, hit her on the face. She climbed on, and managed to pull the canvas over her head as he had done. She looked up and saw his boots still climbing the mast.

'Well done, Cloudier!' he called. 'Now you're on the inside!'

Cloudier looked around her, and gasped. She was, of course, inside the main balloon. Once her eyes had adjusted, she was surprised by how much light there was. Everything was suffused with the red colour of the canvas, but she could see a long way. The space was truly vast – a cathedral of canvas. It was warm – she could see, far away across the curve of the lower edge of the balloon – the great hole where it was attached to one of the funnels that she was used to walking round on the deck of the Galloon. This was the hot air funnel that brought heat up directly from the great boiler below, to heat the air that gave the Galloon its lift. Another funnel on deck was not attached to the balloon, and brought smoke out from the furnace that made the heat. More than the warmth and size, though, she was astounded to see that there were things in here. As she climbed, a small flock of birds flitted past her, squeaking. There was a criss-cross of struts inside the balloon, keeping the tension, so that the space felt almost like an organic thing. Cloudier had the sense that she was inside some gigantic lung, or a dusky forest. Some of the struts had things hanging from them, like strands of hair, or vines. Still climbing,

Cloudier craned her neck round to see all around, and swore for a second that she saw something trot past below, like a deer glimpsed through trees at dusk.

'Impressive, in't she?' called the Captain over his shoulder.

'Amazing!' called Cloudier.

'That's not the half of it, you know!' he said.

'There's more?'

'Yep – watch this. And, for your mother's sake as well as yours, I should point out that what I am about to do will look for a moment as if I am going to die. Rest assured that I am not. Your mother has a tendency to tell me off when I do things that might give you the heebie-jeebies.'

'Sorry about her,' said Cloudier, and managed to flick her fringe across her eyes moodily, even while marvelling at the joy of being alive.

'Not at all. Your mother is . . . or rather would be, if . . . that is to say,' said the Captain. 'Oh, squidink and boondocks, never mind that. Watch this.'

And the Captain fell off the mast. He just stopped holding on, and fell backwards. He passed Cloudier, and spun lazily over as he dropped towards the 'floor' of the balloon.

Cloudier knew better than to call out or scream. She turned herself round as best she could to see where he landed. She thought maybe he would bounce back up past her, as if he were on a trampoline, but he didn't. He hit the canvas, quite a long way out from the mast, and his feet seemed to stick. The canvas stretched and rebounded like the trampoline she had envisaged, but the Captain's feet stayed attached to it. Once it had settled, he lifted a foot and Cloudier heard a tearing sound. Then he began to walk away from her, repeating the noise with every step. The balloon, was, despite its size, a kind of fat sausage shape, which meant that to walk where the Captain was walking should have been like walking up a hill. He should have got only so far, then slipped down to the bottom again, like a towel in a tumble dryer. But he didn't. Cloudier could hear him whooping. He picked up speed.

'Do it, Cloudier! Fall off the mast!' came the Captain's enormous voice, dulled by the vast space.

'Okay!' said Cloudier, who knew better than to question the Captain where this kind of thing was concerned.

She stood up on the little metal rung, and fell backwards as she had seen him do. She flipped over in the air – something here inside the balloon seemed to make it easier to do such things – and landed on her boots. The canvas beneath her bowed outwards, and she laughed at what that must have looked like from the outside. Then she began to walk as he had done. Something about the canvas made her feet stick just enough to stop her from slipping, but not enough to make it hard to walk. She looked ahead, across the inner surface of the balloon, to where the Captain was now just a small figure disappearing into the network of struts. Another shape, a four-legged flitting shadow, ran past between Cloudier and the Captain, and disappeared behind some trailing vines.

Cloudier felt elated, and even here made an effort to suppress it, for the look of the thing. She slouched along for a couple of steps, her long dress dragging on the floor, before breaking into a run. She could now see the floor was slightly spiky, like the burrs that stick to clothes when you walk through the woods. It began to curve upwards after a short while, but it was, bizarrely, no harder to run. As she reached the first of the internal spurs, she looked back and saw that she had travelled partway round the curve of the balloon, though she still felt like she was standing on the ground. Ahead of her the Captain was now singing in a loud basso profundo.

'Let's go fly a balloon, up to the bally moon,

Let's go fly a balloon, and catch my broooothhheeerr!'

Cloudier smiled, and ran faster to catch him.

'What are these . . . animals trotting about?' she asked him, as she pulled alongside.

'Ah! The Bloondeers? A gift from the Sultan of Swoop, many years ago, when the Galloon was new. They usually live inside a gigantic flower called the

41

Gasblossom. But the Galloon suits them well, they've thriven. Throve. Thrived?' said the Captain. He seemed as jolly as Cloudier had ever seen him, though she was sure it wouldn't last.

'They take no looking after. They eat this stuff, the Liken. Grows like billy-o, helps make the gas that keeps the place afloat. It's not just hot air, you know – this is a delicately balanced ecosystem.'

'Wow,' said Cloudier. 'I had no idea.'

'No. Only your mother and I know about them, really.'

'And Isabella?' said Cloudier.

'No,' said the Captain as they walked. 'I never got round to telling her all about the Galloon . . .'

'I'm sorry!' said Cloudier, and her chalk-coloured cheeks reddened slightly.

'Tish! I've thought of a few things I didn't talk to Isabella about. Odd, really.'

He clapped his hands, as was his way when he wanted to change the subject. Nearby, a couple of Bloondeers scampered away.

They walked for a good while longer, and talked about many things. Cloudier was astonished, as she had been once or twice before, to find that the Captain was actually quite talkative, when time and duties allowed. She learned a lot about the ecosystem inside the balloon, and how it was in danger of getting out of balance because there was no-one with the time and expertise to manage it. She also learned a little about the Galloon itself, and what the Captain intended to do with it once his quest to find his lost bride was complete.

'There's people in this world who need a bit of fun, Cloudier, not to mention a square meal and a comfy bed. I've got plenty of each of those here, through no fault of me own. I feel perhaps I can help.'

After what felt like an age, the Captain pointed ahead. They were out of the forest of beams and spurs, and ahead of them Cloudier saw another great bundle of poles, like the mainmast, coming up through the floor of the balloon.

'What's that?' she asked. 'Are we back where we started?'

'Ha! No,' said the Captain. 'We've come halfway round the inside of the balloon. This is where the mast meets the top of the balloon. I don't often get a chance to show off something new about the old Galloon nowadays, so I hope you don't mind the detour.'

'Not at all – but how can this be . . . ?' asked Cloudier.

They were now standing by the mast, and Cloudier's mind whirled as she looked up. The mast was straight and true, and receded into the misty distance as she stood staring up at it. A long way up, it was obscured by Liken and the balloon's supporting struts. She simply couldn't get her head round the idea that she was somehow on the top inner surface of the balloon, standing upside down.

'It's the gas,' said the Captain. 'We need it for a balloon this size to be able to support the Galloon, but it has some odd effects on perception, gravity, time and so on. And the sticky canvas of course – if you were to jump now, you would come back to rest where you are. But once you get outside, you'll see the truth of what I say.'

The Captain reached down to where the canvas met the mast, another rubber seal making the join tight. He heaved on it, and Cloudier felt a rush of cool air on her legs.

'So – get ready for your mind to whirl a little,' said the Captain. 'And, Cloudier – thank you. I rarely get a chance to talk to such a good listener.'

'But . . . I feel we've wasted time . . . the Sumbaroon . . .' mumbled Cloudier.

The Captain put a hand on her shoulder, and looked her in the eye.

'We have to get up top to look out for the Sumbaroon, and this is the only way to do it, with the weather balloon out of operation and all the flying machines needed elsewhere. And if we cannot talk as friends while we walk, then what is the world coming to, eh?'

Cloudier felt a little lump of pride and sadness in her

throat, as she often did when with the Captain. But immediately he was down on his knees, heaving once more at the point where the balloon hugged the mast.

'Go through, Cloudier, and watch your step. Everything's a bit knees over noses out there.'

Cloudier bent down and squeezed through the gap, as when they had entered the balloon an hour – or two – or three – ago. Outside the air, almost as still as the inside, was bitingly cold. She pushed a leg through the tight gap, and found a rung.

'Hold on tight!' said the Captain. Cloudier's last image from inside the balloon was of him smiling and holding back the canvas for her. Then the world flipped around, and she had to hang on for all she was worth to keep from falling up into the clouds and out into space forever. No – down. She would have fallen down. But she could tell from the weight on her arms as she clung to the little metal rungs, that down was now, somehow, above her head. The canvas closed around the mast, and Cloudier clung crazily to the tiny little handholds, now on the section of the Great Galloon's mighty mast that stuck out of the *top* of the balloon, hundreds of feet above even the crow's nest. Like a kitten stuck in the curtains, she gingerly manoeuvred herself round until her feet were down by the balloon and her head was in the air. Above her were just a few feet of mast, topped with a long, flowing pennant, in bright orange and yellow. Above that was a bright figure, an eagle with wings outstretched, standing in a golden nest. The Captain emerged behind Cloudier, like a massive grogram-clad baby being born, and righted himself as she had.

'To the eagle's lair!' he cried, and carried on climbing. 'You can see the world from up there!'

Cloudier followed him.

'And, perhaps, your bride-to-be in the Sumbaroon!' she added.

'Yes! Yes, of course. Onwards!'

Able Skyman Abel was, not for the first time, a tiny bit ashamed of himself. He had spent most of the stormy days deep inside the Galloon, keeping a vital eye on the warmest, comfiest, least wind-battered places he could find, such as the kitchens, his own bedroom, and the space between the funnel and the bakery, where you could lie still and listen to the throb of the boiler, with the smell of new buns in your nose.

So now Abel was doing what he did best, which was overseeing. Overseeing, on this occasion, involved standing at the very front of the Great Galloon, where the starboard rail met the larboard rail. (Abel prided himself on being about the only person on board who knew that 'starboard' and 'larboard' meant 'left and right', although he was also relieved, because he wasn't sure which was which and he didn't want some smart alec pointing it out to him, thank you very much.) So he stood at the pointy end of the Galloon, one foot to larboard, one foot to starboard, or possibly vice versa, and oversaw the tiny flotilla that was going to try and tow the Galloon out of the Dumps.

He fought off a strange urge to tell everyone he was king of the world. Abel could hear voices, a long way off but audible in the utterly still air, that told him someone was, for once, doing as he had asked. The splash had been made by a boat being lowered from a pulley on the sta . . . right-hand side of the Galloon, a short distance behind Abel. He watched it pitch a little on the sea, and then settle.

'Easy there!' he cried, through his megaphone, more out of a need to be involved than anything else.

'Skyman Abel, sir!' came a voice that Abel recognised as that of Jack Clamdigger, the cabin boy who was, in his opinion, getting ideas above his station.

'That's Skyman Abel, *sir* to you!' he called back.

'Erm, that's what I said,' called Clamdigger.

Abel ran the conversation through his head again, and rallied well.

'With the *italics* next time, please! I can tell, you know. Anyway – out with it, lad. What is it?'

'Will you be leading the towing party, *sir?*' called Clamdigger.

'Ha! Will I ever!' cried Skyman Abel, who hadn't thought about it until just that moment. But yes – this could be the way to show his mettle. To lead the party which would pull the Galloon out of the Dumps and back into the reliable Winds of Change. And into the Captain's favour.

'I should coco, young man! Not many like me for putting my back into some honest toil! Away boat three, by the way.'

Now Abel had hopped down and was making his way towards the short wooden crane which was lowering the boats. A small crowd of Gallooniers was standing around it, watching boat three receding.

'Already gone, sir,' called Clamdigger.

'Wait for orders next time, Clamdigger. Guessing 'em is just showy.'

'Aye aye, *sir*,' said Clamdigger, with a roll of the eyes that Abel only half noticed. One of the other Gallooniers let out a little laugh. Abel assumed he was intimidated by the presence of such a senior officer.

He spun round on one shiny boot-heel, and carried on spinning by mistake. He grabbed a rope to steady himself, but sadly it was the one that was currently lowering boat three to the sea. It dragged him with remarkable speed up and over the pulley, then slammed him on the deck at Clamdigger's feet. The Gallooniers laughed again. Abel leapt up, and cracked his head on boat four, which was being readied for lowering. The small knot of men and women gave a small round of applause, and stood around as if waiting for more entertainment.

Abel gathered himself, and spoke forcefully through teeth gritted against the pain of his bumped head.

'I shall pilot goat free,' he said, his clenched jaw perhaps taking some of the power from his words.

There was a slight snigger, but not from Clamdigger – he was now standing to attention, something Abel thought he did all too rarely, and then not well.

'That is to say, I shall . . .' he began again.

'Pilot boat three, sir,' said Clamdigger.

'I don't need your help!' snapped Abel. 'But yes, I will pilot boat three. I think we need some experience at the . . . sticks . . .'

'Oars, sir,' said Clamdigger helpfully, as he continued to wind the lever that was lowering boat two.

'Oars,' said Abel. 'I think it fitting that I should be the first into the boats, where I can lead the towing operation and oversee the operation to tow the Galloon out of the Dumps . . .'

'Well, it needs doing, sir, but I don't mind . . .' began Clamdigger, whose face had coloured up.

Shame at his naked lust for glory being exposed, Abel thought. He snatched a rope from Clamdigger's hands, and the little circle of onlookers widened slightly as everyone took a step back.

'Well, my boy, you're not the only one who can abseil into unknown seas, with the fate of the ship in his hands . . .'

Abel was trying to clamber over the taffrail as he spoke, and was aware that his ceremonial sash, sabre, baldrick, bugle and staff of office were getting in the way.

'And all for no reward except the knowledge of a job well done . . .' he continued, absent-mindedly. He was astride the rail now. He peeked over the edge, and was aware that the sheer size of the Galloon meant there was still a long way down.

'. . . your elders and betters, I shouldn't wonder . . .' he rambled automatically, wondering now if this was a good idea. Clamdigger was tying ropes into a complex safety harness, and trying to attach it to Abel as he lay splayed along the rail.

'Are you okay, sir?' asked a crewman.

'Of course!' snapped Abel. 'I'm pefectly at home, man. I've been doing this since before I was born. Er, you, that is. You've been doing this . . .'

Again Abel was conscious of losing the thread. He looked at Clamdigger.

'So I just climb over the edge into nothingness, and half clamber, half fall, carefully paying out the rope as I go, hoping that nothing goes wrong, and trusting to my crewmates to save me if it does?'

'That's it, sir,' said Clamdigger, testing the harness he had tied, 'and back in time for tea.'

Abel swallowed. He had begun to wonder whether there was a way to hand the job back to Clamdigger without losing face. He was just about to pretend to faint, when that way presented itself.

From one of the little funnels that protruded from the decks around the Galloon, a small blue face appeared, followed by the attached small blue person, and then a pinker person. As Abel paused in harnessing up, he watched them run towards him.

'Ah!' he said. 'I fear perhaps I am to be prevented from leading the expedition . . .'

But as the two figures arrived at the circle of Gallooniers, the blue one with the fur was already talking.

'Clamdigger! Are we glad to see you! We need to find the Captain!'

'We heard the Sumbarooners talking!' said the pink one, which Abel knew was related to the Countess, and so should be treated with grudging respect. He dropped the harness to the ground, and stamped a foot to get their attention.

'I am the superior officer here!' he barked at the children.

'Oh, cod liver oil,' cursed the pink one. Ranterson or some such, wasn't it?

'Hello, Able Skyman Abel,' said the furry blue one with the absurd little horn sticking out of its head.

'Hello, Able Skyman Abel indeed.' Abel stepped out of the harness, and pushed his way through the circle of people to stand in front of the two small Gallooniers. 'I'm terribly sorry, Mr Clamdigger, but it turns out that you will simply have to gird your loins and abseil into the boats yourself – I cannot be expected to do every little thing. Screw your courage to the sticking place, as they say, and get down there. It looks like I must take Strangely and Rallentando to see the Captain.'

'Yes, sorry, Clamdigger, we need to go straight away,' said the scruffy girl-child sincerely. 'You'll have to make do without Skyman Abel's help.'

'Sorry?' said Clamdigger, who was halfway over the rail. 'Oh dear. We'll have to get by somehow. Abseiling party, take the strain, lower me gently, two tugs for faster, three to bring me back up, follow in pairs, on my call, three, four, go!'

The group of onlookers, now looking even to Abel's eyes like a well-drilled work party, had their backs to them, and were calmly going about their business.

'Worry not!' called Abel. 'I shall be back to oversee the towing later!'

No-one responded. Probably awestruck, Abel decided.

'Well then, Stumpy and Razmatazz, what's this

nonsense you've made up about listening in to the Sumbaroon? It won't do, you know, making things up just to get in the Captain's good books.'

And with the warm feeling that something could surely be made of this to help ensure his promotion, Abel put an arm on each child's shoulder, and led them towards the Captain's cabin.

'Good grief,' said the blue one.

Down in the Captain's cabin, Stanley and Rasmussen were locked in. On the way there, they had told Abel all about the Sumbaroon, and the Great Brown Greasy Rococo River. Once in the cabin, he had sat them down, and pretended to go off to the toilet. As he had left, he had locked the door behind him, and called through the keyhole.

'Let's see who gets promoted now then, eh?! I don't know how you know it – I won't be repeating all that poppycock about hearing the Sumbarooners talking! Ha! But I can't wait to tell the Captain where his brother is going!'

Rasmussen had shrugged, put her feet up on the Captain's desk, and helped herself to some ship's biscuits out of the Captain's personal biscuit barrel.

Stanley was a tad more concerned.

'I don't care who tells the Captain where the Sumbaroon is heading, as long as *someone* does, and soon,' he said.

'Abel will,' said Rasmussen, spraying crumbs across the Captain's desk. 'He thinks he'll get promoted.'

'What to?' said Stanley. 'Able Skyman isn't even a thing, he just made it up. What next, Squadroon Leader? Bloon Leftenant?'

'Major Gasbag,' said Rasmussen, idly flicking through a big book on the Captain's desk. 'What's an "Atlas"?'

'Book of maps,' said Stanley, searching round the doorframe for any hidden key, or secret handle.

'Urgh!' said Rasmussen. 'Been there, wiped my feet on that!'

'Maps! Not mats!' said Stanley.

'Ooh!'

Stanley heard the shuffle and rattle of paper as Rasmussen began to look through the big book she had found.

'Do you think that's really the Grand Sumbaroon we keep hearing on the Examinator?' asked Stanley. 'It's never let me hear anyone but Mother before.'

'Don't know – it could be. But it could be a

dastardly trick of some kind. Whatever it is, it's one of the two important things we need to get to the bottom of.'

'What's the other?' said Stanley.

'This biscuit barrel. Have a Mustard Cream.'

'Err, no thanks. What else is there?'

Rasmussen delved deeper.

'Salted Milk, Indigestives, Farty Rings, Witch Tea, spare door key . . .'

'Yuk,' said Stanley. 'Grown-ups like weird biscuits.'

'Yup,' said Rasmussen. 'Look here – the Great Brown Greasy Rococo River.'

She was poring over a page in the atlas. Stanley, absent-mindedly taking a Dead Fly biscuit from the barrel, leaned over to look. He saw a great double-page spread of a beautifully coloured map, hand drawn and covered in the notes and scribbles of a number of previous owners. Here and there were little inscriptions such as 'Here Be Dragons', which some stickler had struck through and replaced with 'There are dragons here'. Elsewhere were equally worrying labels such as 'The Lost City of El Bravado'. Most of the page was coloured dark green, and labelled 'The Uncharted Forest'. Through it ran the wide brown ribbon of the Rococo River.

'This,' said Rasmussen, 'is more useful than a doormat.'

'Yes,' agreed Stanley. 'Unless you want to wipe your feet.'

Rasmussen gave him a Look.

'It's got the sea on it too,' said Stanley. 'Look, we must be here.'

He pointed to a line on the map that said 'The Dumps' in a curly script. Underneath it in bolder writing: 'Here Goes Nothing'.

'I think the Captain would like to see this!' said Rasmussen. 'But we're stuck in here, at the whim of Skyman Abel, unable to get to him, with no way out and no idea where he is! What are we to do?'

'Use the Squeaking Tube to find out where the Captain is, then unlock the door with the spare key from the biscuit barrel, and go and see him to save our good names?' said Stanley.

'Oh, okay,' said Rasmussen, holding up a little brown stick. 'I always say that stopping for a biscuit is the best way to get things done. Chocolate Toe?'

Up in the crow's nest, Cloudier was looking at the world. The sea was still mirror-calm. Above the Galloon was a cloudless sky. Beside her, the Captain was scanning the horizon with his long brass telescope.

'Hmmm,' he said. 'I'm disappointed, Cloudier. I felt sure that with the sea this calm, we'd be able to see the Sumbaroon if she broke surface anywhere between

56

here and Horizon Island. Maybe she's better at staying under than we thought.'

Cloudier was disappointed too. With a hand over her brows, she squinted pointlessly all around.

'What next then, Captain?' she said.

'Well, I wonder,' said the Captain. 'Unhook the tube, would ye, and hail the towing party?'

'I'm not sure how to "hail" anything . . .' said Cloudier, feeling young and ignorant.

'Oh, by Cripes, I'm sorry. "Hail" in this instance just means "talk to". I don't know why I didn't say that in the first place.' The Captain smiled at her and went back to scanning the horizon.

'Err . . . crow's nest to towing party?' said Cloudier, uncertainly, into the cone.

Immediately a distant voice came back up the tube.

'Towing party standing by, sir. All boats fully manned and womanned. Skyman Kollick reporting.'

'Oh, er hello, Mr Kollick. How's Jemima?'

'Fine, sir. Thank'ee for asking.'

'I'm not a sir, you know. I'm . . .'

'Miss Cloudier Peele. I know that, sir. Awaiting instructions, ma'am. Miss.'

'Well, they're not instructions as such, but I believe there may be a little job or two . . .'

'Of course, ma'am, sir, miss. May I say that it would be an honour to take instruction from the Conqueror

57

of the Northern Ice, the Kraken's Friend, the Lookout to Watch, The One Who Flies into Fire, ma'am, sir.'

'Err, yes, well he's right here by me, so . . .'

At this point, the Captain put a hand over the end of the Squeaking Tube.

'He means you, Cloudier. Your voyage into the volcano is a thing of legend among the crew. Do not be surprised if you are treated as a master skymariner nowadays!' he said.

He smiled, and took the tube from Cloudier's hand.

'Mr Kollick, tell the towing party please to take the strain. We must get out of the Dumps as soon as possible,' he said.

'Aye, Cap'n. Which heading, sir? Which way would you like us to tow the Galloon?'

'Well, I should think . . . that is . . .' said the Captain, the telescope to his eye again. He seemed to Cloudier to be searching for any reason to choose one direction over another in this featureless world.

'I was damn sure we'd see something by now . . .' he muttered.

'Sorry, sir?' said Kollick at the other end of the tube.

'Cloudier, do you have a preference? North, Thataway, Roundabout, Windwards or Pell Mell?' The Captain was looking at her, almost hopefully, and holding up the small pocket compass on which these directions were etched.

'I think . . .' began Cloudier, who had decided to

choose 'Pell Mell' for no other reason than that she liked the sound.

But she didn't need to choose anything. At the end of the tube, a kerfuffle was occurring. She heard Kollick saying 'just wait your turn, you jumped up . . .' and then the voice of Skyman Abel piped up.

'Captain! This man is resisting a superior officer!'

The Captain, to his credit, did not tut or roll his eyes. Cloudier did though.

'Abel,' said the Captain. 'Mr Kollick was just awaiting our ideas on which way to go . . .'

'Never mind that!' yelped Abel, apparently still scuffling for control of the tube. 'I know which way we should go! The Grand Sumbaroon is heading . . . For the Great Brown Greasy Rococo River, over!'

There was a pause. Cloudier looked at the Captain, who seemed to have found something interesting in his ear.

'Er. Right,' he said, pulling whatever it was out of his ear and flicking it away.

'The Great Brown Greasy Rococo River!' said Abel. 'That's Left-by-Your-Left of here! Towing party, set course immediately!'

'No,' said the Captain quietly. 'Don't do that. Cloudier, what do you think?'

Cloudier was, as ever, astonished to be asked, but did her best to formulate a sensible opinion.

59

'I've heard the Rococo River is hugely wide, Captain, but I'm not sure it would be deep enough for the Sumbaroon.'

'It is! They're blinking going there, you stupid girl, over!' said Abel's tiny voice.

'Abel,' said the Captain. 'That's the last time you'll use that word to any member of the crew.'

'Yessir,' said Abel, suitably chastened. 'But it's the truth! I know it to be true, over!'

'I suppose it's possible,' said the Captain. 'But it's mighty dangerous territory around there. The Uncharted Forest has barely been mapped, the river is treacherous . . . we lost passenger Perky Luffington there, of course. And then there are the rumours . . . over . . .'

'Never mind the rumours! Your brother is heading there now, with your bride-to-be in his evil clutches! Please, Captain! For Isabella! Over!' squeaked Abel.

This seemed to galvanise the Captain slightly.

'I need no persuading to put myself in danger for her sake,' he said. 'But many times now have I endangered the lives of those around me. I would not do so again without very good reason. Why do you suspect they are heading that way, Abel, over?'

'I . . . just . . . think . . . they are . . .' said Abel, as if trying to talk while lifting up a filing cabinet full of lies.

'Well, if it's no more than a hunch . . .' Cloudier

heard herself saying. The Captain looked at her appraisingly, and then at the tube.

'Yes. Skyman Abel, thank you for your thoughts. But if you have no further proof, then I cannot . . .'

'I heard Stanley Crumplehorn and Marianna Rasmussen talking about it, over!' he admitted, almost hysterically.

Aha, thought Cloudier; *so you know their names when it really matters*.

'They heard someone talking on the boy's infernal long-distance listening machine. Over,' said Abel, as if it was the hardest thing he'd ever said.

Immediately, the Captain raised his voice to what Cloudier thought of as 'command level'.

'Mr Kollick!' he said. 'Instruct tow party to head "Left-by-Your-Left", please,' full speed ahead for the Rococo delta. First person to spot land gets extra trifle. Abel, ask Stanley and Rasmussen to meet me in my cabin, if you would – no, on second thoughts, in Stanley's cabin, if he doesn't mind. Thank you. Anstruther out.'

He put the tube back into its cradle. He once again had about him the look of a man consumed by one thought, and not entirely aware of anything else. But he took a moment, as he climbed out of the crow's nest, to look at Cloudier.

'Thank you once again, Ms Peele,' he said. 'I return

to the deck. You may stay here if you wish and do what you do so well – look out for the Sumbaroon.' He handed her his telescope, hopefully.

'Aye aye, Captain,' said Cloudier. The Captain smiled, and ducked out of sight.

Familiar feelings of pride, fear and excitement welled up in Cloudier. She put the telescope to her eye – it wasn't very romantic or poetic, but she'd love an extra dollop of trifle come dinnertime.

The Great Galloon was on its way again.

Two days later, Stanley and Rasmussen were in Stanley's bedroom, listening once again to the Examinator. They had been more or less glued to it since their meeting with the Captain, when he had asked them to keep track of any unusual goings-on on the airwaves.

Stanley found it hard to know what was unusual and what wasn't. He had been using the Examinator to communicate with his parents ever since he had become a member of the Galloon's crew. His mother gave him lessons twice a day, alongside a number of other children who were spread around the world, in places too remote for them to attend school the normal way. But this was a regular appointment, so Stanley rarely just tuned in to see what he could hear. Until now, that is. And it was an education, to say the least. He and Rasmussen were slightly starry-eyed, and surrounded by empty tea mugs and sandwich plates. She had one hand on the dial, tuning and retuning it with a glazed intensity. He was lying on his back on the floor, staring at the wooden beams that ran across his ceiling. For the past forty-eight hours, Stanley had been keeping a note of the things they had heard, in case anything turned out to be useful. It read:

00hrs 11mins Strange crunching, munching sound coming from the Examinator. Machinery of some kind?

00hrs 17mins White noise. Rasmussen very tetchy. Need restorative bacon sandwich.

00hrs 47mins Back from the mess. Definitely ready now for long, uninterrupted listening.

08hrs 47mins Wha? Jus' woke up. Woss goin' on?

08hrs 48mins Refreshed after quick 8hr nap, now really ready to listen out for anything suspect.

08hrs 49mins Nothing.

08hrs 50 mins Voices!

08hrs 51mins Turns out it was Mother. Time for

lessons. Rasmussen laughing at me.

15hrs 19mins Beautiful, haunting music – must be picking up whale song somehow.

15hrs 21mins Not so beautiful music now – Rasmussen snoring. She's got no stamina.

15hrs 22mins 32nd cup of tea of the vigil so far. Best yet. That should keep me awake for agkvkjcfjhgvjkb . . . .

And so on. In a nutshell, they had heard nothing, except a few snippets of conversation between ships on the ocean below, some whales and dolphins, and Stanley's mother telling him all about the Square on the Hypotenuse, wherever that was. But Stanley was determined that they should continue. Rasmussen wasn't so sure.

'We should be out there, seeking here and seeking there, seeking the Sumbaroon everywhere!' she moaned for the umpteenth time.

'We will. But we can be a vital part of knowing where Zebediah is going. We just have to listen out.'

'But nothing's happened!' said Rasmussen. She rarely whined, but when she did, she made up for lost time by being the whiniest person since Little Whingey Martin, the Grouchiest Boy in Moansville.

'Well, that's perhaps true. But maybe there's a pattern. Let me see your notes,' said Stanley.

Without looking up, Rasmussen tossed him her notepad, which was purple and smelled of lavender. He flipped the page, and saw what she'd written:

All listening and no adventuring makes Stanley a dull boy.
All listening and no adventuring makes Stanley a dull boy.
All listening and no adventuring makes Stanley a dull boy.
All listening and no adventuring makes Stanley a dull boy.
All listening and no adventuring makes Stanley a dull boy.
All listening and no adventuring makes Stanley a dull boy.
All listening and no adventuring makes Stanley a dull boy.
All listening and no adventuring makes Stanley a dull boy.
All listening and no adventuring makes Stanley a dull boy.
All listening and no adventuring makes Stanley a dull boy.
All listening and no adventuring makes Stanley a dull boy . . .

'Is it all like this?' asked Stanley.

'Yes,' said Rasmussen. 'Except for some of page fourteen.'

Stanley turned to page fourteen. In the middle of the page, alongside the same sentence repeated over and over again, was a picture of Stanley, with a speech bubble coming out of his mouth. He was saying 'What am I? A monkey or a unicorn or an alien or an abominable blue snowman?' Stanley was used to this from Rasmussen, and he was about to close the book and give it back, when he noticed something at the bottom of the page.

'Hello, hello, anybody out there?' it said.

'What's this?' he asked Rasmussen. He showed her the page.

'It's you, wondering whether you're a monkey or a . . .' she said.

'Not that! This!' snapped Stanley, unwilling to have the 'what creature is Stanley' conversation for the seventy-second time.

'Oh,' said Rasmussen, picking crumbs off a plate she found under Stanley's bed. 'That's nothing. Just a conversation I heard over the Examinator while you were asleep.'

'Wha?' said Stanley, agog.

'What are you doing?' asked Rasmussen.

'I'm being agog!' said Stanley.

'No you're not. Agog means "very eager to hear something". What you're doing is more "astonished".'

'Oh. I'm both astonished and eager to hear something. Is there a word for that?'

'Yup. Agognished.' Said Rasmussen. 'It looks like this.'

She pulled a face of astonishment while cupping a hand behind each ear.

'Okay. This?' said Stanley.

'Yup. That's agognished alright.'

'So?' said Stanley.

'So what?'

'I am agognished to hear that you heard a conversation on the Examinator while I was asleep. Let's read it.'

'Oh, right. Yes. I'll be the girl. She seemed nice.'

Stanley held up the book and they read the conversation.

Girl: Hello, hello, anybody out there?

*Boy: (grumpily) Of course there's no-one out there.
We're forty fathoms underwater. Come away
from the window.*

Girl: Okay, let's try the wireless again then.

*Boy: I could have sworn I heard someone snoring
just then.*

Girl: A snordfish?

*Boy: Maybe. Hello, hello, is there anyone out there
who isn't a fish?*

*Girl: Nope, nothing again. Best cover it up again
    in case the Boss comes in.*

Boy: Captain Zebediah? Or . . . her?

*Girl: No, she's too busy on the bridge, poring over
    that map of hers. Looking for El Bravado, and
    getting cross with everyone no doubt.*

Boy: Well, they do call her the 'Irate Queen'.

*Girl: 'Pirate Queen', Ragnarsson. They call her
    the 'Pirate Queen'.*

*Boy: Oh. Right. That makes more sense. Sorry,
    Sidney. Cup of tea?*

Stanley put down the notebook.

'Corks,' he said. 'We'd better tell the Captain about
this. The Parrot Queen indeed. We'll have to watch out
for her stealing our nuts and so on.'

'"Pirate Queen", Stanley Crumplehorn. It says
"Pirate Queen",' said Rasmussen.

'Oh. Right. That makes more sense. Sorry, Rasmussen.
Cup of tea?' said Stanley.

'Yes,' said Rasmussen, 'but then we definitely should
go and tell the Captain, straight away.'

'Oh yeah!' said Stanley. 'Straight after tea.'

'And a biscuit,' said Rasmussen.

'Of course! And maybe a quick game of snakes and
hopscotch.'

'But then we'll tell him straight away.'

'Definitely. Won't waste a moment.'

As she spoke, Rasmussen twiddled a nob on the Examinator. Stanley knew she meant to turn it off, but it went the wrong way, and a noise caught their attention. A rhythmic thumping noise. It was like the sound your heartbeat makes in your ears when you're embarrassed or worn out, except that it changed tempo, and occasionally paused, in a way that would have sent Stanley running to a doctor if his heartbeat had done anything similar.

'Thump-a-Dang-BonkBonk. Thump-a-Dang-CLANK Bonk. Thump-a-Dang-BonkBonk. *Pause* Ker-Dang-Bonk Bonk-DerDUNK!'

'Hmm,' said Rasmussen, her ear pressed to the little square of mesh where sound came out. 'It sounds almost like . . .'

'STANLEY DEAR, ARE YOU THERE? IT'S YOUR MOTHER CALLING! TIME FOR LESSONS!'

This last came through at an earsplitting volume, because Rasmussen had turned the heavy brass knob round to eleven. She flung herself onto Stanley's bed, and slapped her hands over her ears. Her face was a picture of terror for a second, and Stanley laughed aloud.

'Oh there you are, dear,' said his mother. 'Something funny?'

'Yes, Mum,' said Stanley, as Rasmussen's face took on its familiar look of thunder.

'Good af'noon, Missus Crumplehorn missus,' she said, in a quick, polite mumble.

'But, Mu-uuum,' said Stanley. 'I'm too busy for lessons! We've got to find the Sumbaroon, and work out what the "Thump-a-dunk noises" are, and who we keep hearing on the Examinator!'

'Very nice, dear, I'm sure,' said his mother. 'But that sounds like the kind of thing the Captain is very good at. We need to run through some lessons. Map reading, traditional percussion music of forest peoples, the geography of river deltas, and electronic engineering , specifically as it pertains to radio waves.'

'But, Muuuuuuuu-uuuuuuuuuuu-uuuuuuuuuuuuuu uuuuuuuuuuuummmmmmmmuuhh!' groaned Stanley. 'When am I EVER going to use any of that stuff in REAL LIFE!?'

Nevertheless, he opened his text book, and turned to a new page.

'Be a good boy, and just listen, dear. Other children are very grateful you know . . .' And so began the familiar litany of the lesson. Stanley knew there was no way he could just sneak out, as Mrs Crumplehorn was good friends with Ms Huntley and a number of other crewmembers. His life would not be worth living. His mood was not brightened by Rasmussen beaming widely at him as she left the room, signing at him as she went.

'I'm going to get a sausage and strawberry sandwich. Enjoy your lesson!'

She closed the door, and Stanley turned back to the Examinator with a sigh.

GOODNIGHT!

Later that evening, in the Galloon's warm and cosy canteen, known to all as the mess because of its comfortingly shambolic air, the crew of the Galloon were gathered. There was very little difference in practice between the crew, i.e. those who were involved in flying the great vessel, and the passengers, i.e. those who lived and worked onboard, but didn't actually pull ropes, consult maps, and so on. But the difference was understood by most, and when the Captain called a meeting, as he had done now, everyone onboard seemed to know whether they should attend or not. So of the thousands of people, animals, creatures, and other things that made a life on the Galloon, a few dozen people were present. Stanley and Rasmussen, though not officially crew, would not miss out on such a thing for all the world, and had doggedly ignored

Abel's remarks about 'minors loitering about the place'. They were making themselves useful by helping Cook hand out glasses of iced punch. The ovens had all been switched off days ago, but the heat in the little room was oppressive nonetheless.

The Captain was striding up and down, his second-best hat bumping against the low beams, his brows knitted in concentration.

'Shall we begin?' asked the Countess, brightly.

'Yes, yes, I think so,' said the Captain. He turned to the assembled throng.

'So – my brother seems to be heading into the very heart of the Uncharted Forest. I have reason to believe that he does not know what he faces – my maps show that we are almost at the base of a waterfall known as Lethal Force, which his Sumbaroon will be unable to traverse. We have the advantage of flight, and so such obstacles do not concern us. When he next surfaces, he must surely realise that all hope is lost. The question facing us is this – why is he risking so much, when it seems inevitable that he is trapping himself in a corner? And what does he hope to gain from heading this way at all? Why not stay in the open sea, where he can evade us much more easily? And when he surfaces and finds himself trapped, how do we proceed to rescue Isabella?'

Stanley, munching a slice of melon, realised that, for

once, he probably knew more than many of the assembled grown-ups about what they were facing. He raised a paw, intending to tell the small crowd about what he and Rasmussen had heard on the Examinator about the Pirate Queen. But before he could do so, the door to the mess opened a crack.

'Who's this? Yes?' snapped Abel in the direction of the door, irritably. 'This is a crew-only meeting, I put a sign on the door. Why can't you just wait a few . . .'

He trailed off as a hand appeared in the crack, and pushed the door open further. 'Hand' was the word that came to Stanley's mind, but it was not a hand like any other. It was a great, shaggy, long-fingered thing, with knuckles like walnuts and jagged, grubby claws where the nails should be. Stanley felt himself tense up, and heard Rasmussen whistle appreciatively as the door opened fully, and the owner of the hand squeezed through the doorframe. It was the only member of the crew who was hardly ever seen in the mess – though as he pushed his way through the door and into the room, he did stop at the great tea urn to fill a cup that looked like a thimble in his mighty grasp. As if unaware that everyone was watching him, he took a genteel sip from the cup, and turned to face them all.

'Oh, don't mind me,' said the Brunt, his voice slightly muffled by the three scarves, balaclava and high-collared coat that he was wearing. 'Please carry on talking.'

There was a moment of pause, as everyone readjusted to having a nine-foot-tall, orange-furred creature in their midst, wearing at least three layers of clothes in the sweltering heat. Then Ms Huntley spoke.

'Welcome, the Brunt! I assume the hot climate, which we all find so oppressive, means that you can move around more freely away from the boilers?'

'Yes, Harissa Huntley.'

Rasmussen whooped quietly, and said, 'Hurrah for the Brunt!' Stanley punched the air. The Captain gave the Brunt a big bear hug, looking for a moment like a little child as he was lost in those great hairy arms and many layers of clothes.

'Well, it's a great pleasure to see you, I must say,' said the Captain once the chatter of welcome had died down. 'We were just discussing our next move.'

'That is why I am here, Captain. I was listening to the drums.'

'Are they distressing you?' asked the Countess. It was well known that the Brunt could not abide loud noises.

'No, the Countess. But I looked out of my little window to see if I could see who was playing the drums.'

'And did you, old friend?' asked the Captain.

'No. But I saw the waterfall.'

'We were just discussing the fact that it will be our

75

friend in trapping the Sumbaroon, when Zebediah makes it this far upriver. We will have him in a corner.'

'No, Captain,' said the Brunt, in his matter of fact way. 'The Sumbaroon is already here.'

'You saw it!?' said the Captain. 'I'm a fool! I should have had someone looking out!'

'You had me,' said the Brunt.

'Yes of course, I meant . . .' fluffed the Captain.

Abel chipped in, irritably: 'Of course he'll be trapped! He's in the Sumbaroon, a fifty-ton metal beast – he can't leap up the blessed river like a migrating salmon, or change into a gecko and scamper up the cliff face!'

The Brunt turned calmly towards Abel as he spoke. Despite his calm expression, the great yellow tusks, gigantic curled horns and deep dark eyes had a disquieting effect on anyone who saw them.

'Er . . . can he?' finished Abel.

'Why not come and look?' said the Brunt.

'Yeah!' said Rasmussen. 'Why not come and look!' The crew did not need to be told twice that if the Brunt thought something was important enough to make him speak in front of a room full of people, it was probably very important indeed. As one and with no discussion, they stood and followed the Brunt out of the mess.

Down in the depths of the Great Galloon, about fifty-five people were cramming themselves, or trying to cram themselves, into the Brunt's tiny little room. The room was right beside the gigantic furnace that made all the hot air the Galloon needed to stay afloat, and so it was an incredibly hot and fusty place at the best of times. With so many people in it, the atmosphere was almost unbearable. Stanley had managed to get to the front of the throng, where the Brunt was pointing out of his tiny, soot-covered window, at something below them in the forest. The Captain was also at the window, and everybody else was doing their best to see what it was they were looking at.

'What is it!?' called Rasmussen, from the back of the crowd. The tone of her voice told Stanley that she was not at all happy about being so far from the action. Stanley tapped the Brunt on the leg, and he picked Stanley up in one hand as if he were a cupcake.

'What can you see?' cried Rasmussen. A few other voices – Stanley recognised Crivens, Tump and the Sultana of Magrabor – echoed the sentiment.

'Ye Gads!' cried the Captain, his voice booming around the little room.

'WWhhaaaaaaaatt!?' yelled Rasmussen.

'Marianna,' said the Countess, quietly.

'Sorry, Mum, but really! Tell us what you can see, Mr Pumplecorn!'

Stanley ignored the slight on his name, and began to describe what he could see.

'There's some sooty old planks, a slightly rotten windowframe, a rusty lock that's been painted over . . .'

'Oh, sorry, Stanley,' said the Brunt. He lifted Stanley slightly, so he could now see out of the window and down to the forest below.

A groan emitted from the crowd, but the Brunt spoke again, as if he and the Captain were the only people in the room.

'I saw the Grand Sumbaroon of Zebediah Anstruther come up the river, and then it stopped in the pool there below the waterfall. I was going to come and tell you, but then I saw that it was beginning to . . . change.'

'Change, the Brunt?' asked the Captain, his steely glare focused on something way below and in front of the Galloon. Stanley followed it, and took a breath. There, only half submerged in the shallow pool at the base of the great waterfall, was the Grand Sumbaroon. It looked battered, rusty, as if it were on its last legs. He told the assembled throng as much over his shoulder.

'It doesn't have legs! It's an underwater craft!' said crewwoman Neela.

'Ermm . . .' said Stanley, who was nothing if not a slave to the truth. 'That was true . . . until now.'

As he watched, sitting on the Brunt's great hand, he was almost unable to believe his eyes. The Sumbaroon, which as far as he was aware was merely a metal vessel riveted together clumsily, began to split along its seam, like a dragonfly emerging from its pupa. First, the back of the great ship began to split. Although they were still a long way away, Stanley could see the rivets popping off, and the great steel plates cracking like an eggshell. He described what he was seeing to the throng.

'Do you mean pupa? Or larva?' said helmsman Monty. He got a stern look in return.

Stanley continued to narrate, as the two halves of the Sumbaroon's shell continued to split apart. From within something newer, shinier, and somehow, bigger, began to emerge. First, a small appendage, like a millipede's leg, appeared from within the broken shell of the Sumbaroon. Then another, and another, until an entirely different craft could be seen. It was long and thin, like a metallic eel, but lined along each side with small jointed legs. It pushed and heaved its way out of the old shell of the Sumbaroon, which was almost literally trodden into the mud. The audience in the Brunt's little room was speechless, listening to Stanley's description of events. The only interjections came from Rasmussen, who occasionally helped with words that Stanley couldn't put his finger on, like 'appendage' and 'unctuously', though Stanley didn't really need that one.

'It's just . . . waiting!' said Stanley. 'Standing in the wreckage of the Sumbaroon just waiting.'

'Not waiting. Growing,' said the Captain.

And he was right. Inside the craft, some kind of

pump or hydraulic system was making the machine grow, in rhythmic pulses, as if it were taking great breaths. Sliding plates in its sides took up the slack.

'It must be twice as big as the Sumbaroon now!' said Stanley, to gasps of consternation.

'Why is it doing this? Who has made it so?' asked a woman who was carrying a small child on one hip.

'Isabella,' said the Captain, quietly.

'Nonsense!' cried Abel, who clearly thought he was being supportive. The look the Captain threw at him was perhaps the angriest look Stanley had ever seen him give.

'I do not speak lightly, Mr Abel,' he said, that word 'Mr' holding more displeasure than a tirade of abuse from a lesser man. 'She is an engineer beyond compare. My brother took years to create the Sumbaroon, a pale imitation of my own sweet Galloon. Only Isabella could improve it so in a few short weeks. She must be working under duress.'

There was a silence, during which the Brunt laid a great hairy hand on the Captain's shoulder.

'Look!' cried Stanley, to which Rasmussen's irritated voice replied, 'We can't!'

'The new vessel seems to be . . . to be standing up, on its dozens of little metal legs!' said Stanley. 'It's rippling them, like an insect would. And now it's . . . yes, it's swimming to the riverbank!'

81

'It will never make it through the dense forest!' cried the Sultana of Magrabor. 'Surely?'

'It's not heading for the forest,' said the Captain. 'It's heading . . .'

'For the Lethal Force waterfall, Captain Meredith Anstruther,' said the Brunt.

Stanley watched, and commentated, as the machine hauled itself out on the rocks, making the assembled crocodiles scatter like so many tiny mice. The great machine, part military tank and part slithering creature, then threw out from its front end a couple of whippy cables with hooks on. They seemed to penetrate the waterfall itself, which was barely more than steam by the time it reached the pool, and cling to the wet rock behind. The thing, which Stanley was already thinking of, and describing, as the 'FishTank', then seemed to be able to climb up the rockface behind Lethal Force. Its legs rippled and moved in waves. Its pair of cables repeatedly threw themselves forward, finding a hold and pulling the craft inexorably upwards.

'What's "inexorably"?' said Kollick, the Captain's no-nonsense steward.

'Er, "unstoppably",' said Stanley.

'Then say "unstoppably". There's no glory in baffling your audience!'

'Sorry,' said Stanley, and continued his commentary.

The FishTank was now a few dozen feet above the

pool, and the battering it was receiving from the water-fall seemed to be doing it no harm at all. Down below, the broken parts of the Sumbaroon, so long the Galloon's entire aim and focus, were being dispersed by the mighty current. It was no more than so much scrap iron.

'How quickly can you stoke us up, the Brunt?' said the Captain, sharply.

'Quickly, Captain Meredith Anstruther. The furnace is still hot.'

'Then I have but one thing to say.'

'Woop woop!' cried Rasmussen, in anticipation. 'Oh – we should tell you about what we heard on the Examinator!'

'Not now, Ms Rasmussen,' said the Captain. 'First this – ALL HANDS TO ACTION STATIONS, IF YOU DON'T MIND HELPING ME OUT ONCE MORE IN MY HOUR OF NEED, THANK YOU KINDLY!'

The great voice filled up the room they were all in, and filled Stanley's head with fear and excitement. The Brunt plopped him carefully on the ground, and loped over to the corner of the room where he kept his tools. The room was already emptying, as the Captain's command/ request was obeyed/ fulfilled.

'While the craft is on the cliff face we have the advantage,' said the Captain to Ms Huntley, who was listening intently. We must try and press that advantage home. If I am not mistaken, at the top of the falls we will find a landscape that even the Galloon will find it hard to fly over.'

'Aye, Cap'n,' said Ms Huntley. 'I studied the maps too, such as they are. We must rescue Isabella before he takes her into the Darts.'

GOODNIGHT!

Getting the Galloon going from a standing start was quite an operation. Before Stanley and the rest of the crew had shuffled out of the Brunt's little room, the huge stoker had already grabbed his shovel and heatproof mask and headed off to begin firing up the great furnace, which would boil the water in the mighty reservoir, which would pump steam and hot air into the great balloon itself, and all the minor outlying balloons. This gave the Galloon its lift, but for forward motion it relied largely on the winds themselves – so the Captain and Ms Huntley had made immediately for the Captain's cabin, where they would study charts and take readings from the lookouts stationed around the Galloon, which would tell them where the favourable winds were likely to be.

Stanley and Rasmussen did not have official roles in the procedure, but they were very good at making themselves useful. Rasmussen went off to watch the main anchors being hauled up, where she often kept morale high by doing a new and innovative dance on the main capstan, much to Abel's annoyance. Stanley made his way to the bows of the Galloon, from where he hoped to get a good view of the Darts, whatever they turned out to be, and perhaps see if he could make head or tail of these drums. He liked to be able to see where the Galloon was going. From the Brunt's room, which had been unknown to most of the crew until Stanley and Rasmussen had stumbled across it a few months before, he squeezed through the crowd, most of whom were heading to the new, automatic lifting platform, which would transport them up the main deck. But Stanley went the other way – to a panel in the wall that looked suspiciously similar to all the others around it. There he tapped three times with his foot, and once with his horn. Then he twisted a brass hook that looked like it was there to hold a lantern. The panel slowly scraped and heaved itself upwards, revealing a shaft like a dumb waiter – but one that had air rushing through it like water rushing through a pipe. Stanley carefully leaned into the tunnel he had uncovered, and fiddled with a small lever on the back wall.

'Not the library . . . not the hospital wing . . .' he said to himself, thoughtfully. 'Here it is – Claude's head.'

He pushed the lever towards the panel with the words 'Claude's Head' and felt the rush of air change slightly. He knew that further up the channel, wooden doors were closing and others opening, so that he would be wooshed along the system of tubes to his chosen destination – Claude, the great winged tiger, a wooden figure that clung to the front of the Galloon, his wings outstretched along her sides. He had used the tubes before – indeed he and Rasmussen had recently spent a fun few weeks getting about this way, thereby infuriating and confusing anyone who didn't know the tunnels existed. The trick was to make yourself fit exactly inside the wooden tube, like a cork in a bottle. Then the pressure would build up behind you, and you would squirt along the tube, to be popped out at your destination, slightly befuddled and feeling like a rat emerging from a drainpipe, but none the worse for wear. He gingerly stepped through the gap in the panels and felt the wind whistling past him. He braced himself against each wall of the tunnel, and tried to fill as much of the space as possible. As the pressure built up behind him, so did the excitement. He took a deep breath, making sure he blocked the tunnel completely – and then he was off.

'Wooooooooooooooo!' he cried.

As the walls streamed past him, he felt the occasional burst of air from a side tunnel that would set him off along a different path. The air was warm – he knew from talking to the Brunt that it came ultimately from the very furnaces that kept the Galloon afloat – and he could almost relax as he shot along. He whooshed past a tiny notice on the wall that read 'Claude's Head – 40 feet'. He braced himself, and almost before he was ready, he felt himself shot out of the tube like a torpedo, and found himself flying right over Claude's stripy wooden head.

'Erm . . .' said Stanley, who was not given to panic. He had that feeling you get when you realise that, although things have always turned out fine in the past, there may be one time when they don't and that this may be that time. Claude's head was big, but not that big – he was over it fairly quickly, still travelling surprisingly fast. He grabbed at one of Claude's great wooden ears as they passed, but couldn't get a finger to it. Then he was looking down at Claude's great tiger face from above. His eyebrows were like ledges in a cliff face. His nose stuck out like a huge wooden tiger's nose. Behind him, Stanley was aware of the unimaginable bulk of the Galloon bearing down on him – but it wasn't bearing down quick enough to save him. He was now out in the wide blue sky beyond Claude – he

felt momentarily like a dolphin playing around the bow wave of a seagoing ship.

Below him, the river rushed not too far away – the Galloon was, by its standards, fairly low, as it hung motionless in the air a few hundred feet from the waterfall. Stanley had a moment to wonder whether he could swim, having never had the urge to find out. Then, as he lost forward momentum, he was tumbling through the humid air.

'Could anybody lend a hand . . . ?' he said quietly, hoping that by some chance the gyrocopter, or even Fishbane the Seagle, might be within earshot.

They were not, it seemed. He fell head over heels over head over heels over head, seeing the green of the forest and the dark shape of the Galloon scooting past his vision in turn. It was almost fun, but with no Rasmussen to share it with, and the certainty of his imminent demise, he couldn't quite throw himself into it.

'Ah well . . .' he said to himself, sagely, squeezing his eyes shut. 'It's what I would have wanted.'

He just had time to wonder about that, and to wonder whether he could talk his way out of being eaten by a crocodile, when a mighty fist, the size of a mattress, grabbed him round the waist. The fist was solid as oak – which, indeed, is what it was made of – and all the wind blew itself out of him as his downward progress was halted abruptly.

'Hoooooooooooofffff!' he said involuntarily. He opened his eyes to find that he couldn't see. He was inside the fist – enormous wooden claws the size of canoes were closed around him – and it took him a moment to realise what had happened.

'Claude!' he breathed.

It was a legend onboard the Galloon that, in times of great danger, Claude would spring to life to save the ship. Stanley had never seen any evidence of this before now – he had stood on Claude's head many times with Rasmussen, and knew it to be made of the same wood as the rest of the Galloon – but now it seemed that it was indeed true. He felt the fist moving, as if he were being lifted up again. Now light flooded through cracks between Claude's huge claws, and he could see the sky, grey and looming, beyond them. The claw opened out like a flower, and Stanley felt the warm air rush in on him again. He was sitting on Claude's outstretched hand, as the enormous tiger held him up for inspection. Claude was still clinging to the Galloon with his other arm, and his wings were still stretched along the vessel's sides. But he was now facing Stanley, and from this angle Stanley could see that the eyes were not dead wooden things carved out of a tree, but bright, thoughtful windows into a living creature's mind. They were sharp and penetrating. It was like being stared at by a lighthouse. Had they always been this way? Stanley didn't know – he had never seen the Galloon from this angle before. In fact, he was willing to bet no-one had, as even the Captain had seemed unsure as to whether the legends about Claude were true or not. Despite feeling more exposed, and more exhilarated, than he had ever felt before, Stanley had a moment of gloating that he, as an incomer to the Galloon, knew something that Rasmussen, who had lived all her life onboard, did not.

'Hello, Claude!' he said. 'Sorry about standing on your head all those times!'

Claude held him closer. He opened his great mouth, and teeth like obelisks parted. Was it a smile? Or was the beast about to speak? Stanley held his breath again, and as if from nowhere, words formed in his mind.

THE GREAT GALLOON NEEDS YOU, SMALL BLUE

Stanley whipped around, as if this could be a trick being played on him by someone else up here on Claude's outstretched hand. He turned back.

'Me?' he said. But no more words came. In fact, Claude's attention seemed to be elsewhere. He was looking past Stanley, in the direction the Galloon was travelling in. Stanley turned again, and saw that he was staring at the Lethal Force waterfall, visible

91

intermittently through the clouds of spray. He saw the FishTank, a little silver eel wriggling and yanking itself up the mossy rockface, behind the flow of water.

'Could you help us catch the FishTank? Rescue the Captain's bride?' asked Stanley, aware that it was perhaps slightly cheeky to ask a favour of a gigantic wooden tiger within moments of finding that he was actually alive.

RESCUE? NO

'Oh,' said Stanley, who was disappointed but not surprised. 'Why have you not spoken before now, if you don't mind me asking?'

BEFORE NOW, THE GALLOON'S DOOM WAS NOT IMMINENT

'Oh,' said Stanley again, who could think of a few times when it had felt imminent enough. 'So, now . . . ?'

IT IS IMMINENT

'And just so I'm sure, imminent means . . . ?'

THE GREAT GALLOON'S DAYS ARE NUMBERED

'Oh,' said Stanley for the third time. There didn't seem much else to say.

TO ONE

'To what?' asked Stanley

THEY ARE NUMBERED – TO ONE

'Oh,' said Stanley, aware that perhaps it wasn't enough. 'One day, eh? Tsk.'

GOODNIGHT!

Cloudier Peele tried hard to be an effete poet. She aspired to a life of art and contemplation. She drank tea made of almost anything other than tea – hyssop and wolfwort, cloudjuice and tinklebane – all of which seemed to taste like leaves boiled in water. She wore floaty, impractically long dresses, and wished she were better at swooning. And yet she seemed to often find herself engaging in derring-do. She had even been known to swash a buckle or two. In her time she had flown her little balloon across icy wastes, into volcanoes, and on all sorts of life or death missions into the unknown. And now she was doing it again. Perhaps it was time for a rethink.

Because of the massive size of the Galloon, it was quite hard for anyone on deck to get a clear view of anything that was directly below them. So sometimes the Captain called on Cloudier to take him out in the weather balloon, for him to better see the lie of the land. And now, as they waited at the top of the waterfall for the FishTank to clamber up, he had called on her again. But this time was different – this time her mother was coming too.

'We've got ropes, compass, the barometer, altimeter, fire extinguishers, inflatable life raft, vacuum flask of iced tea, and all the charts I could find,' said her mother, clambering over the rail and into the little basket.

'What kind of tea?' asked Cloudier.

'Just tea, dear,' said Ms Huntley. 'That's the only kind of tea there is. Anything else is just leaves boiled in water.'

'Hmmph,' said Cloudier, although she was secretly relieved.

The Captain was next. He leapt over the rail, and made the little balloon shimmy and shake.

'By criminy, but it's hot, is it not?' he said, conversationally. Cloudier noticed that he had taken off his greatcoat, and was wearing linen britches. But the hat remained – albeit his second-best hat, his first having been stolen by his brother.

'It is. And those drums . . .' said Cloudier's mother.

They all listened for a moment.

'Thump-a-Dang-BonkBonk. Thump-a-Dang-CLANK Bonk. Thump-a-Dang-BonkBonk. *Pause* Ker-Dang-Bonk Bonk-DerDUNK' went the drums, as they had been doing ever since the Galloon had crossed the bay.

'I don't know,' said the Captain. 'They're insistent,

for sure – but they don't sound like a threat, if you ask me. And besides, what can threaten us up here in the mighty Galloon?'

Cloudier was surprised to hear the Captain sounding relatively upbeat, but then perhaps he was confident that his bride's rescue was imminent.

'Let's go and see what my dastardly brother is up to now,' he said, and his face seemed to darken again.

'I think he must be heading for El Bravado,' said Ms Huntley, poring over a map as Cloudier began to pump hot air into the balloon above them.

'Yes,' said the Captain. 'The Lost City of Silver. Legend tells of untold treasure just sitting there for the taking – though I suppose you'd need to approach by air to stand a chance of getting there. It's damn strange, as he's never shown the least inclination to wealth in the past. He's no pirate. Its power he craves, it seems, and poor Isabella of course.'

Cloudier looked at her mother, who rolled her eyes in an almost imperceptible way at the Captain's tendency to secrecy.

'Hold tight, we're off!' said Cloudier, as the little balloon pulled away from the deck of the Galloon.

'It's good to have you onboard, Harissa,' said the Captain with a smile. Cloudier just had a moment to think this a little strange, before they were away and over the rushing river, watching it plunge hundreds of feet over the cliff edge. The clouds of spray thrown up by the falls were surprisingly refreshing.

'Take her down!' cried the Captain over the roar of the falls. 'How close can we get to the waterfall?'

'Within safe and sensible boundaries!' said Ms Huntley. 'And do not roll your eyes at me, my girl!'

'Oh, Mother!' said Cloudier. Calling her mother 'Mother' was something she was trying out. She was concerned it made her sound more like an old-fashioned school mistress than a world-weary but cultured young woman, but it was early days yet.

'Please don't call me Mother,' said Ms Huntley. 'You sound like an old-fashioned school mistress.'

So that was that.

They descended away from the Galloon, where Abel was officially now at the helm, though Clamdigger was doing the actual steering. Its size never ceased to astound Cloudier – but she had to concentrate on flying her own little craft. The Captain's great legs took up a lot of the space in the basket, and her mother was perched on the little bookshelf where Cloudier kept her tiny library. This, along with all the safety equipment Ms Huntley tended to bring along since the small incident when Cloudier flew alone for hundreds of miles across a frozen landscape before landing in a volcano, left very little room for Cloudier to manoeuvre. But she managed to handle the burner, and the little string that controlled their altitude, with one hand. Another of Clamdigger's many recent improvements around the Galloon was a tiny little outboard motor-propeller for the weather balloon, so that it was nowadays not entirely at the mercy of the winds. Cloudier had the tiller of this little put-put engine in her other hand, and she used it to steer them towards the waterfall as they fell slowly towards the cliff face.

'Woah!' said Cloudier. 'I mean . . . how exquisite they are!'

She pointed at the waterfall, where little fishes, like bejewelled ribbons, were clinging to the rock face, and occasionally making heroic upwards leaps against the current. They seemed able to stick to the rocks like sticky tape, but nevertheless their efforts must have been exhausting.

'Tinselfish!' said the Captain.

'Beautiful things!' said Ms Huntley.

'Indeed,' said the Captain, and the look they gave each other gave Cloudier such a shock that she didn't even think of writing a poem about the beautiful fish and their uphill struggle.

'Erp . . .' she said uselessly, and then had to jerk the handle of the little outboard motor sharply, as a shape came flying out of the mist below them. It was one of the FishTank's hooked cable-arms, searching for a purchase on the rock.

'Not meant for us, I don't think!' said the Captain, as they lurched away from the cliff.

'No – but we should be careful nonetheless!' said Ms Huntley. 'Here it comes!'

As the cable found a purchase on the mossy rocks, the rest of the FishTank came into view. They were so close they could hear the whirring and clanking of hydraulics as it hauled itself against the relentless current. It was a shiny thing, almost as beautiful as the tinselfish, its overlapping panels shining as it shrugged the water off. Almost before they had seen it, it was past them, as Cloudier had to flash the burner to bring them alongside again.

'ISABELLAAAA!' the Captain suddenly yelled, making Cloudier and her mother jump out of their skins.

'Meredith!' snapped Ms Huntley. 'I know this is hard! But if she were able to hear you, she would not be able to do anything about it. We must remain calm.'

'I have remained calm for many months, as my brother holds my beautiful bride against her will! How long can any man hold these things inside? I must save her!'

And to Cloudier's astonishment, the Captain seemed ready to leap from the balloon onto the FishTank, where he would certainly be thrown off by the current and dashed against the rocks below.

'Up, Cloudier!' called Ms Huntley.

'No! Keep her steady!' said the Captain.

Cloudier, without so much as a moment's thought, brought the balloon up and away from the FishTank.

'Cloudier!' said the Captain, aghast. But then he turned and saw the looks on the faces of his companions, and was quiet.

'We can't let you blunder into a foolish accident,' said Cloudier's mother calmly. 'You will be no use to Isabella if you are smashed to pieces down there.'

She pointed down to the base of the falls, where the churning water and razor-sharp rocks meant certain death for anyone who fell in.

'No, of course, you are right. We need a plan . . .' said the Captain. 'Thank you as ever, Harissa, Cloudier, my moments of . . .'

'Enough! When we are safe back onboard the Galloon, just the three of us, then you may say what you wish . . .' said Harissa.

'Four of us,' said the Captain. 'Isabella will be there too.'

'Of course,' said Ms Huntley. Cloudier saw her look at her feet, as she did when she wasn't saying everything she wanted to say.

'Look!' said Cloudier.

The FishTank was almost level with them again, and was now very nearly at the top of the falls. But it had stopped, its two cables clinging to rocks right at the edge of the falls. In its back, where the dorsal fin would have been if it had really been a fish, an opening was appearing. It wasn't anything as crude as a hatchway – silver panels slipped over each other to reveal a circle, which irised open silently. A head poked out of the opening, while the silver panels rearranged themselves into a kind of dam to hold the worst of the water off.

'Zebediah!' roared the Captain, and Cloudier saw his fists clench and his knuckles whiten.

Ms Huntley leaned over to Cloudier, and spoke calmly.

'What have we got that we could fire into that hole? A flare? Anything?'

'No!' said the Captain. 'Please, my Isabella is somewhere within.'

As the Captain spoke, Cloudier saw his brother, who was the dead spit of him in almost every way, raise a loudhailer to his mouth.

'Brother!' he called.

'You have no brother!' called the Captain, whose voice was so powerful that no loudhailer was necessary.

'Err . . . I do. You! And Tobias,' said Zebediah.

'Oh yes! How is Tobias, do you know?' called Meredith.

100

'Fine, fine. Mother says he's doing very well. He's been promoted to regional manager!'

'Good! Good for him. But you do not have me as a brother. I am your mortal enemy, nothing more, until you release my bride, and make reparations for your conduct!'

'Yes, I see – but no, I can't do that!' said Zebediah. It seemed to Cloudier that he was listening to somebody, or something, down below, in the main body of the FishTank. 'I have to tell you . . . I mean . . . I want to tell you something. Merry?'

The Captain was visibly startled.

'I am not Merry to you! Only Mother may call me that!'

'And Tobias?'

'Yes, of course and Tobias! Regional manager, you say? Well, well.'

'Yes! He gets the corner office, company steam wagon, the works.'

'Hurrah for him, eh?' The Captain jerked himself out of a reverie again. 'But – you say you must tell me something? Make it quick, for my Galloon is not far off, and will make short work of you!'

'You will not take any action against me while Isabella is onboard. I know that well enough, so your threats are idle ones. Just listen, for once in your life, to your younger brother!'

'Just say your piece!' snapped the Captain.

'She . . . I mean . . . I will not tolerate being followed any longer. I have brought you here for a number of reasons, but one is because it is the one place in the world where your Great Galloon may not follow. Once I am at the top of these falls – which I will be in a matter of moments – your life and your ship will be in graver danger than they have ever been before. Your door is imminent. Do not follow me to El Bravado. I repeat – do not follow me to El Bravado.'

'My door?' said the Captain.

'What?' called Zebediah.

'Did you say my door is imminent? That doesn't make sense.'

'Well – it's what the Pirate Que— I mean, it's what I want to say. Make of it what you will.'

'Where's my hat!?' called the Captain.

'What?'

'Where's my best hat? You stole it. Why aren't you wearing it? You never could look after things.'

'Well, it's a pirate hat, and I'm not a pirate. I stopped wearing it.'

'It's not a pirate hat! It's a Captain's hat, you lowdown lubber!'

'Black, three corners, red ribbon at the back – that's a pirate's hat in anyone's books. I gave it to the Pirate—'

102

Cloudier was now watching Zebediah very closely, looking for any opening they could exploit. As the grown-ups argued about hats, she noticed a hand, holding a piece of paper, reach up from inside the FishTank and tap Zebediah on the leg. He flinched, then took the paper and read it. The Captain and her mother were looking at each other, aghast about the hat revelation, so didn't notice.

'Doom!' said Zebediah. 'Not door. Your doom is imminent.'

'Oh!' said the Captain and Ms Huntley together. 'That makes a lot more sense.'

'So do not follow!' cried the Captain's evil brother. He ducked back down into the FishTank, and the strange portal closed behind him.

'How dare he threaten me? Back to the Galloon, Cloudier. I have seen that parleying will get us nowhere. We must stop him once and for all.'

'But what did he mean about the Galloon being unable to follow?' asked Cloudier, as she lifted the balloon away from the waterfall again and back towards the Galloon, which was still moored a half-mile or so behind. 'What's at the top of the falls?'

'It is certainly a strange landscape,' said her mother. 'The sharp, unnavigable rocks known as the Darts, with the river winding through them. Beyond that it's largely uncharted. But there's the myth of El Bravado, the Lost City of Silver, which seems to be driving Zebediah onwards.'

'But the Galloon has been there before – we used to have a passenger who was born round here; young Perky Luffington. Dropped him off at home, just a few miles from here, years ago. The Galloon crossed the Darts then, no problem. I shouldn't like to crash into one, and we may have to stay lower than we'd like, but any talk of our imminent door is highly fanciful, even by Zebediah's twisted standards.'

'Doom,' said Ms Huntley.

'Yes, of course.'

They floated for a short while in silence, as the roar of the waterfall fell away, and the thumping of the drums became audible again.

'I wonder what happened to old Perky?' said the Captain, almost to himself.

'He may still be around here somewhere, but we'd have no way of contacting him. The chances of bumping into him are a million to one,' said Ms Huntley.

'You're right, of course. As you always are,' said the Captain. It seemed to Cloudier that he and Ms Huntley gave each other another of what could only be described as One of Their Looks.

Stanley was, contrary to expectations, very much enjoying being held in the mighty fist of a tiger. Claude had not spoken again, and had gently closed his fist once more around Stanley's body so that there was no possibility of escape, but somehow Stanley understood that this was for his safety, rather than through any malice.

If only my friends could see me now! Stanley thought to himself. *Rasmussen, or Clamdigger, or . . .*

CLOUDIER

Stanley had decided not to wonder how Claude did that – it was either science or magic, and either way there was very little he could do about it. He looked up at the tiger, and saw that he was looking past Stanley, off to the right. Stanley followed his gaze, and saw the little weather balloon, returning to the Galloon. Its tiny engine popped and spluttered as it gained height, clearly aiming for the main deck. It looked to Stanley as if there were three people onboard. He waved, and shouted, but they were too far away, and probably focused on negotiating the outriggers and balloons that made any approach to the Galloon problematic.

'Can you call them?' he asked Claude, but got no response.

Stanley waited a few minutes, as there seemed little else he could do, then spoke again.

'Could I please go and have my dinner now? Could you put me back on the Galloon?'

THE DEMISE OF THE GALLOON IS IMMINENT

'Yes, so you said. So . . . may I go and warn the Captain?'

THE CAPTAIN HAS BEEN WARNED

'Okay. So I suppose he'll want to . . .'

But before Stanley could continue, the great tiger and his enormous fist gave a mighty lurch.

WE ARE UNDERWAY

'Ah, okay. I'd really like to go back onboard . . .'

YOU ARE SAFER HERE

'Safe?'

NO

BUT SAFER

'Ah,' said Stanley.

They were indeed underway. Stanley twisted in Claude's fist, and saw that they were slowly picking up speed as they moved towards the waterfall. The FishTank was now nowhere to be seen – Stanley suspected it had clambered over the top of the cliff and headed off into the mysterious landscape beyond. The Galloon rose sharply as it picked up speed. Overhead, thunder rolled – the air had been so humid for the last few days that rain had seemed certain – and here it was. Fat drops landed on Stanley's head. The spray from the waterfall combined with it, to soak his fur and skin. Behind him, Claude growled, a long low rumble that mingled with the thunder. Stanley felt it rattle through him, and was overjoyed once more at his life on the Great Galloon.

They were now coursing through the sky, over the waterfall, which they skimmed so close that it seem to Stanley as if the great rudderboards that reached out below the keel of the Galloon must surely have been in the water momentarily. Fish flipped from the water as the Galloon's enormous shadow passed overhead. Stanley was enjoying the sight so much he almost forgot they were in hot pursuit – and then he saw the FishTank. The river here widened out almost immediately, until it was spread out across a wide plateau. It snaked and twisted through rocks and boulders, many of which were shaped like great grey space rockets ready for launch. The FishTank was half swimming, half clambering among them – pulling rocks over with its long whip-like cable arms, to make a passage for itself. Its captain clearly didn't care what destruction he wrought in this magnificent place – if something was in the way, he smashed it down or threw it aside. Colonies of birds flew away just in time as the awful contraption knocked down the rocks on which they had made their homes. Many of the rocks were covered in a kind of hanging moss that seemed to weight them down – and as one particularly huge rock formation was cracked and thrust over by the manic contraption, a very strange thing indeed happened. Stanley noticed that much of the moss was hanging not down, as you would expect, but up into the air, like the hair of someone who was hanging upside down. The green trailing tendrils seemed to be reaching into the sky. As the rock was shouldered aside by the FishTank, the weird green moss seemed to take its weight. And rather than falling over, the rock began to float slowly up into the sky.

'What the . . . ?' said Stanley, as the strangeness of what he was watching overtook him.

Another moss-covered rock broke from its moorings, and began to float majestically upwards, for all the world like a party balloon, albeit one that was heavier than a house and as sharp as an axe.

'We're going to hit them . . .' said Stanley, thoughtfully.

YES

A pause.

SO PERHAPS YOU ARE NOT SAFER HERE AFTER ALL

'Ah. Then maybe you could drop me back onboard?'

TOO LATE

There was a tearing sound, to go with the rain and the thunder and the splintering of rock. Claude was ripping his wings free of the Great Galloon's wooden sides. His other hand also came free, and he stretched and flexed his fist as if he had slept on it funny. Then, as nothing was connecting him to the Galloon any more, he dropped like a stone for a few feet. Stanley's heart leapt into his mouth, a place it was getting quite used to finding itself in. Claude held onto him tightly but gently, even as he stretched out his phenomenal wings, and beat them once.

'Well, this is something to write home about!' said Stanley, happily.

Claude flapped his broad wings once more, and Stanley tried not to think about the fact that they were, as far as he knew, still made of wood. They were no longer in danger of falling, and Claude began to outpace the Galloon. He flew straight towards the great spur of rock that was now almost directly in the Galloon's path.

'Down there!' cried Stanley, as a smaller piece of rock that must have been dislodged earlier came into view just below them.

GRATITUDE TO YOU

Claude lashed out with an enormous leg, and smashed the little rock to pieces. Some fell to the ground, others, with the odd moss attached, flew up past them. But none were now big enough to harm Claude or the Galloon.

The big rock ahead was now almost at the same height as the Galloon, but Stanley had no way of knowing whether the Captain would see it, and if so whether he would have a chance to avoid it.

'Faster!' he cried, then put his hand over his mouth, embarrassed to have spoken so to someone he had just met.

URGENCY UNDERSTOOD

They did indeed speed up, and Claude soon had his shoulder to the great rocket-shaped boulder that threatened the Galloon. He shoved and heaved, but even his enormous strength didn't seem able to move it far enough off course.

Stanley looked back, and watched the Galloon approaching. It seemed to him that somebody onboard had noticed the imminent danger, as the huge vessel was in the beginnings of a turn to larboard. But in this still air, with no wind behind, turning the Galloon could be a pretty slow process, and Stanley didn't think they would get out of the way in time. Far below and ahead of them, the FishTank was still on its way, smashing and destroying as it went. Looking back he could see little figures moving around the deck of the Galloon, moving sails, pumping balloons, and generally trying anything to change course. It was not going to be quick enough. He stared at the rock that Claude was throwing all his weight against.

'The moss!' he cried. 'Get the moss off! Then the rock will sink again!'

PLAN APPROVED

With his one free hand, Claude began to tear the long tendrils of moss from the rock. As he let them go, they shot into the air, but the rock didn't seem to be sinking out of harm's way.

'Put me on there!' called Stanley. 'I can help!'

NO SAFETY THERE

'No safety here if the Galloon is destroyed!' cried Stanley.

POINT TAKEN

Claude gently held Stanley between two of his mighty claws, and gingerly plopped him onto the very top of the floating rock, where the moss was thickest. It felt rubbery and unpleasant to the touch, but Stanley began yanking and pulling at it as quickly as he could. Claude now had both paws free, and soon Stanley began to feel as if they were making a difference. The rock's upward progress was halted, but it was still in the path of the Galloon, which was now careering crazily towards them, sails flapping monstrously from every yardarm. Stanley guessed that a full stop had been called.

'More!' he cried, and renewed his efforts to tear the strange, seaweedy substance off the rocks. He took great armfuls of the stuff and flung it into the air with gay abandon. He had the feeling that the rock was beginning to drop. He looked to the tiger, who also seemed, strangely, to be almost enjoying himself. As Claude took one more great armful, the rock started to plummet to the ground. Stanley whooped with relief, as the Galloon's prow, now Claudeless, passed a few feet over his head. Then he realised he was now on a rock that was no longer covered in whatever floaty substance had kept it in the sky. Claude seemed to realise the same thing, and he threw himself backwards off the rock, grabbing Stanley and flipping wildly over in mid-air to avoid smashing into the Galloon. He did so just in time, as the rock fell to earth and shattered into thousands of glass-sharp pieces. But there was no time to celebrate – Claude threw his wings wide and flew ahead of the Galloon once more, to where more rocks were threatening to make the prophecies of the Galloon's demise come true.

This is fun! thought Stanley. *I wonder what Rasmussen's up to?*

Rasmussen had gone straight from the meeting in the Brunt's hot little bedroom to Stanley's bedroom, where she had been busy at the Examinator. She had expected to hear Stanley's mother ready to give him lessons, but strangely she was nowhere to be heard. Rasmussen was not a fan of the Examinator – anything that had been invented mainly to make lessons unavoidable was never going to be on her list of 'favourite things I ever heard of' but she had a strong feeling that it would be useful in the current circumstances. She felt bad that she had not been able to tell the Captain what they had heard previously about the Pirate Queen, but there was no proof as yet that they had been listening to the Sumbaroon – it could of course be anyone pretending, or fantasising, about being onboard Zebadiah's vessel. It was imperative that she find a way to talk back to that mysterious pair, the boy and girl who had seemed to be speaking from inside the Sumbaroon itself. She was keen to find out if they were who they said they were.

'Hello, Nora,' she said, as the little fat rat stared at her unblinkingly.

Rasmussen had the feeling that Nora didn't like her, but she didn't let that put her off, as she took a small screwdriver from a toolbox on Stanley's bedside table, and began to unscrew the back of the Examinator. She may not go to lessons very often, but that didn't mean she didn't know a thing or two . . .

Up in the wheelhouse, Cloudier, the Captain and Ms Huntley were cheering at the tops of their voices. They had seen the flying rocks, of course they had, but all their efforts to change the Galloon's course had been in vain. They had resorted to calling for a full stop, which meant loosening all the sails on the Galloon, and letting them flap in the wind so there was no forward motion at all, but their impetus had carried them on. Just when they had felt sure they must crash into the strange floating rock that had been sitting in their path, something incredible had happened. A great brown shape, like a version of Fishbane that was a thousand times bigger and carved from oak, had flashed out from beneath the Galloon in a shower of shattered rocks, and flown off into the distance, where it had begun to smash, shove and heave a path through the rock field for the Galloon to follow. It was also, Cloudier saw, taking the opportunity to fling a few rocks at the ground, where she presumed the FishTank was still making its way towards the horizon.

'Go Claude!' yelled the Captain, pumping his fist with delight.

He and Ms Huntley gave each other a hug and slap on the back.

'Mother!' cried Cloudier, embarrassed.

'Oh, shush, Clouds,' said her mother, which was her usual response.

Cloudier couldn't help being elated as well, as she watched the great creature slamming its way through the ever-growing cloud of rocks.

'We'll have to go slow, but I think we can proceed,' said the Captain. He grabbed the nearest Squeaking Tube and cleared his throat.

'Ahem, Skyman Abel, Mr Clamdigger, I think we can risk half-speed ahead with caution. Follow that tiger.'

A tiny squeak told Cloudier that at least one of them had responded.

'Tiger?' she said, nonplussed. 'Claude? Not . . . *Claude* Claude?'

'Yes indeed, Cloudier. It seems the legends are, in fact, true. Who knew?'

'Not even you?' asked Ms Huntley.

'On this occasion, I promise you, not even me. I was given the figurehead – Claude – as a gift. I did not watch him being carved or installed. I knew the rumours about him, but thought that was what they were. It seems not. It seems we have a powerful ally.'

'Where was he when we nearly lost Clamdigger to the sea? Or when we had to fly into that volcano?' said Cloudier, thinking aloud.

'Oh, shush, Clouds,' said her mother.

They looked again through the wheelhouse window and there was Claude, crashing a fist into one of the smaller rocks, which was smashed to smithereens by the blow. Again some of the pieces flew straight up into the air, and some fell to the ground.

'It's Liken,' said Cloudier, quietly.

'What's that?' asked the Captain, tearing his eyes away from the tiger's heroics.

'It's Liken that makes the rocks float – like inside the main balloon.'

'Stall me engines, you're right!' said the Captain. 'I've never seen it grow naturally, but it can be nothing else. How strange the world is!'

'When have you been inside the main . . . ?' asked Ms Huntley, but she was interrupted, as the great shape

116

of Claude came rushing back towards them. They watched in awe as he thumped through the air directly in front of the Galloon, smashing a few remaining small rocks as he went. He roared, and even over the rain and thunder, they felt the power of his voice.

MISSED ONE

They all felt it, like a message being projected on a wall inside their minds. For Cloudier, it appeared in a strong, tombstone script, as if carved in stone. She marvelled at the feeling of it so much that she almost forgot to pay attention to the meaning.

'Missed one what?' she asked of the world in general.

Claude came to a dead stop crouched on the deck of the Galloon, as if he were a sprinter at the start of the race. He somehow managed to avoid all the lines and debris. One fist was raised towards the wheelhouse, and they were amazed to see it had Stanley in it. He was plopped gently onto the poopdeck in front of the wheelhouse, then Claude collapsed in a heap, as if exhausted.

'Missed one rock,' said Stanley, pointing upwards towards the main balloon, before flopping to the ground, bedraggled and spent.

Cloudier followed his finger, and saw a shard of rock, perhaps as big as a horse, floating upwards between the deck and the balloon. A few hands were standing around, jaws agape at the sight of their giant

117

lucky mascot sprawled headlong on the deck, and a few more were watching the rise of the rock splinter. It was shaped like an ancient hand axe, and Cloudier knew that when it reached the balloon it would cut through it just as effectively as any axe. She grabbed a Squeaking Tube, and turned its little dial to 'Broadcast'.

It was strange to hear her own voice echoing all around the Great Galloon. Especially as what it was saying was this:

'The Galloon is going down. We are about to crash land in the Darts. All hands to brace positions. BRACE! BRACE! BRACE!'

'Well done, dear,' said her mother as she crawled under the control console in the wheelhouse and put her head between her knees. 'Such presence of mind.'

'Oh, shush, Mother,' said Cloudier, secretly proud of herself.

In Stanley's bedroom a few minutes before, Rasmussen had been screwing the back cover back on to the Examinator. She had switched a few wires around, and tightened a couple of connections, as she had read about in *The Little Adventurer's Guide to Electrickery*. Then she had taken out some bits of hay and poo that Nora had obviously left in there on one of the occasions when he had been let loose in Stanley's room. Now, she hoped, she would be able to choose who she spoke to and who she heard rather than relying on chance.

She sat in front of the machine and began to twiddle the dial marked 'Twiddle This One', which was usually used only to make the voice of Stanley's mother sound clearer if she was a little faint. But now the machine had a much greater range of frequencies available to it, and Rasmussen began to listen carefully as a series of voices dribbled out of the mesh.

'. . . *welcome to super sounds of the seventies, this next record is by Bob Wisdom, who is seventy-nine* . . . *by gum I wish there was someone out there to listen to this* . . .'

'. . . *fishbite forty, rising to seventeen later, good. Long heggarty, Gale force two, falling, strong later* . . .'

'Come on come on come on . . .' said Rasmussen, who was not the most patient of people. She carried on twiddling, and eventually found what she was hoping for.

'. . . *trying to contact the Great Galloon of Captain Meredith Anstruther* . . . *This is Magdalena Ragnarsson, onboard the Sumbaroon 3000, calling anyone who may be able to get us in contact with the Great Galloon . . .'*

Rasmussen jumped and put her mouth to the speaktophone.

'This is me!' she cried excitedly. 'I'm on the Great Galloon! I think we have to say over, over?'

'Haha! We do! I told Sidney we'd get hold of you eventually! He's such a gloomy gus! Over!'

'I know someone like that! Over!' said Rasmussen, jumping up and down now with glee at her success.

'We have to get a message to your captain! His brother has made a terrible mistake! He wants to put things right but he can't! Over!'

'What?' said Rasmussen, suspicion returning. 'Why can't he? He just has to let Isabella go, and say sorry! Over!'

'That's just it!' said Ragnarsson. *'He tried to let her go – she doesn't want to! Over.'*

Rasmussen took a moment to digest this, and then decided it was a cruel trick.

'You Sumbarooners! You're all bad'uns! I've half a mind to . . .'

But she never had a chance to find out what she had half a mind to do, because at that moment, all communication was lost, as a Squeaking Tube began to blare out its frightening message across the ship:

'BRACE! BRACE! BRACE!'

120

'Oh poo,' said Rasmussen, as she grabbed Nora and went to hide under the bed.

The crash of the Galloon into the forest of the Great Brown Greasy Rococo River was, perhaps, the loudest thing ever to have happened there. The people who lived in the forest, the players of the drums, had long memories. They knew the names, occupations, peculiarities and peccadilloes of their ancestors back to the umpteenth generation, which was a lot. They had tales of things that had happened long before the forest had grown up, when the rocks were mountains, and the river a mere trickle in the dust. But nothing had made quite such an impact on the area as the crash of the Galloon. It came down in among the rocks that they knew as 'The Pimples of Great Rococo', but which they knew were more widely known as the Darts. Ari, who had lived his whole life around the top of the waterfall, had been watching with interest as these strange contraptions made a meal of climbing up the cliff face and over the rocky landscape. Were they angry demons? Creatures from the Pre-Waking years, escaped from their midnight domain to wreak revenge on the mortals once more? Or machines built by people from far away, who had come here in search of the untold material wealth of El Bravado?

Probably the latter, Ari decided. When he watched the flying tiger fight and destroy the rock Darts as no-one had ever done before, he waivered a little, but then decided that even he probably wasn't a demon, as demons didn't exist. It was news to him that flying wooden tigers existed, but it was clear that they did.

So these were people from far away, and not just far away as in 'over in Coracle Bay' but far away as in 'from a different country'. He only knew one person who knew much about things that were that far away. So he watched the almighty vessel plummet to the ground in a barely controlled way, smashing rocks and rending trees as it came. Then, when the silence descended, he hopped on his bounce-stilts and went to get Perky.

Onboard the Galloon there were, by some miracle, no casualties. The balloon had indeed ripped like a wet hanky when the rock went through it, but the Captain and Ms Huntley had managed to control the descent to some extent, and many of the Galloon's outflyers – the gyrocopter, the biplane – had got airborne with as many people as possible onboard before they had hit the ground. Most of the others had taken refuge in the ballroom, or other rooms in the centre of the ship, so that although a few sharp rocks had made holes in the sides, and many sails were ripped and ropes snapped, the damage was far less than it could have been.

Now, almost an hour after the impact, with the light fading, the Countess was out in the gyrocopter looking for help, Ms Huntley was trying to ascertain exactly where they were, and the Captain and Skyman Abel were assessing the state of the ship.

'Absolutely in tatters, sir, from bow to stern,' Abel was saying, struggling to keep his voice from cracking. This was not how things were supposed to go, he felt.

'Yes – it is a worry, Abel, but again we must be grateful . . .'

'That no-one was more seriously hurt, sir, yes, you said. And despite the fact that I myself sustained a nasty graze to the gluteus maximus, I . . .'

The Captain interrupted him with a look.

'Gluteus maximus?' he asked.

'Bumcheek!' said Stanley, helpfully.

'Yes, thank you!' snapped Abel. 'Despite that, I feel that, for his own good, we should take young Clamdigger to task, as he was on lookout duty at the time of the –'

'Rigging can be fixed. Grazed bumcheeks . . . gluteus maximuses . . . heal. The Galloon will fly again one day, and I for one am thankful beyond measure that we have not fared worse – but for now I must work out what needs doing to achieve that aim, and how we go about doing it. Will you help me do so, or do you feel an urge to speak of blame and recrimination, petty upsets and minor grazes, Mr Abel?'

'Oh. I. Well. It's just,' said Abel, pathetically. 'I'm not sure I feel well, sor—'

'Come come, Abel, not the time to be shirking, I should say?'

The Captain was looking at him askance.

'No, of course, it's just . . .'

Somewhere a treefrog chirruped, and Abel jumped like a sneezing kitten.

'I think it might help you to chip in and get some work done,' the Captain was saying.

'But . . . something feels wrong, sir. They're closing in . . . I don't feel I could be of use . . .'

'Very well. Then tell me – what grade is that rope there, that binds the jibb'loon to the outrigger?'

'17d, sir, though we're out of it in stores. I know we've got a fine load of 12e, which is much the same but with a thicker core. Could easily be pressed into service for that job, no doubt . . .'

Abel heard himself saying this, and realised the Captain had done it again.

'Then do so, Abel. And I shall start to think of the greatest problems we face – namely, repairing the main balloon, and refloating the old tub.'

'And rescuing Isabella, sir?'

'Yes, of course,' said the Captain, slowly. 'Of course!'

'Of course I'll do what I can, sir. But it's the trees, see, and the rocks. They're . . . listening sir. Closing in, as it were. There are ears all around. They can see us, but we can't see them . . .'

124

Abel felt his eye twitch, just once.

'Ears all around? They can see us, eh?' said the Captain.

'Yessir!' whispered Abel, fighting an urge to hide behind a tree.

'With their ears, eh? Damned clever people, if you ask me. They should come out and say hello.'

And with that, the Captain strode off, probably to see where he could be most useful. Abel watched him go, and then slowly hid behind the mast.

In the forest, not so very far away, among the great rocks and the looming trees, Ari found Perky Luffington. He was the only person capable of making sense of the great city in the sky that had fallen among the rocks and trees. He had been born here in the forest, but had spent many years abroad, and now had some ways that his local friends and family considered eccentric. He was currently sitting at a small table outside his palm-leaf-clad home, drinking a long fizzy drink with lemon in the top, and eating cucumber sandwiches with the crusts cut off.

'What-ho don' cher know, old fruit!?' he cried, on seeing Ari. His little fingers were extended so far that he was in danger of falling over. He put down his newspaper – which Ari noted was over three months out of date – and stood up. He was wearing a threadbare three-piece suit, with the trousers cut off at the knee, and the sleeves at the shoulder. He had not forsaken the black bowler hat, though he had cut a hole in the top of it to let the heat out.

Ari was unfazed by his bizarre appearance. It was well known that those who went off to find work and opportunity abroad usually came back, but that they usually came back changed. It was known as 'town fever'. It didn't seem to do any harm as such, but a number of Ari's acquaintances would wake up at the same time every morning, don unsuitable clothes, and then wait on a platform of their own construction for a steam train that would never arrive. Perky was often known to complain about a game called 'cricket', but when pressed was utterly unable to explain the rules. He had come back to the forest a number of years ago now, and had settled down very well, except for these few strange oddities.

Ari shook his hand, and accepted his invitation to sit. He even accepted a sandwich.

'I need you to come and see something,' he said, while Perky poured him a glass of the fizzy stuff. 'You know that noise that seemed to shake the earth apart last night?'

'Noise, old boy? Do you mean the drums? Just some friends of mine, chatting,' he said, raising an eyebrow.

'The noise! The noise that was definitely the loudest thing ever heard anywhere. It shook the trees, sent rocks flying into the sky, burst the eardrums of anyone standing within a mile?'

'Oh yes, I do recall a kerfuffle of some sort,' said Perky.

'Kerfuffle? Does that mean "noise like the world is ending"?' asked Ari incredulously.

Perky cocked an eyebrow.

'Meteorite, was it? Earthquake, perhaps?' he said, while slathering thick cream onto a scone that was already slathered in jam.

'It was a great flying canoe the size of a mountain, all sails and ropes and bits of wood, falling to earth and crashing among the Darts.'

Perky's demeanour changed – his eyes widened. He dropped his scone. All pretence left him. He took off his home-made pith helmet and laid it on the table.

'Ari,' he said, in a voice that was much less high-faluting. 'I used to live on that thing. My friends are on it. Could you take me there?'

GOODNIGHT!

The Galloon crash site was a hive of activity. The ship had come to rest on a kind of platform of rock, almost

127

hanging over the edge of the canyon through which the river thundered, smashing against the great moss-covered rocks. Stanley had disembarked, for the first time in a very long time, and the feeling of rock beneath his feet was an odd one. Another odd thing was that he was standing, out in the open, alongside the Brunt.

'It is just about warm enough for me here, Stanley Crumplehorn. And I need to find dry wood for the burners – the coal scuttle was smashed during the crash, and all coal lost to the great rushing river Rococo,' the Brunt had said.

He was wearing a great quilted coat, given to him by the Captain, and the biggest slippers Stanley had ever seen, while nearly everyone else was in shorts and shirt sleeves. But he was here, and it made Stanley's heart glad. Together they stood, a few hundred feet away from the craft that they both called home, and regarded it anew.

'What an incredible thing she is,' said Stanley.

'How lucky we are,' said the Brunt.

'Thanks, you're not so bad yourselves!' piped Rasmussen, emerging from the undergrowth with a grin. She had the Examinator strapped to her back like a knapsack, and had managed to find half a coconut with a straw in it. She slurped the juice noisily.

'Not . . . oh, never mind. Let's help find supplies – we need to look out for tall straight trees, vines for

ropes, and a hundred other things, Clamdigger says . . .'

'Yes, we could do that . . .' said Rasmussen. 'Or we could head out into the forest to find out who's playing these drums?'

'But, shouldn't we do what we've been asked?' said Stanley.

'Where's the fun in that?' asked Rasmussen.

'It's not about fun, it's about taking some responsibility for your actions, Marianna Rasmussen,' said Stanley.

Rasmussen, the Brunt and Stanley all looked at each other for a moment. Stanley cracked first, doubling up with mirth.

'Hahahaaaaa! I nearly had you there!' he cried.

Rasmussen splurted coconut water over his shoes as she laughed too.

'Hahahah! Responsibility for . . . for . . . for . . . ahahahahah! Good one!'

The Brunt laughed too, a great harrumphing chortle that sounded like some huge beast of the undergrowth greeting the morning.

'Good one, Stanley,' he agreed. 'You are a playing card.'

'I vote we wander off in a random direction, in the hope that whatever we bump into will end up being useful in some way,' said Rasmussen.

'That usually works!' said Stanley.

At that moment, Skyman Abel stepped out of the undergrowth behind Rasmussen. Stanley didn't know whether he had sustained some kind of blow to the head (again) during the crash, or whether the heat and stress were just getting to him, but he had abandoned his starchy uniform, and was now wearing trousers with lots of pockets in them, a dirty vest, and a piece of rag tied round his forehead. Still being Skyman Abel though, he had clipped his medals to his chest.

'Aha!' he drawled, in a strange voice that wasn't his. 'Looks like we got ourselves a bunch of deserters! Gonna give away our positions, are you?'

'We're going to try and find the drummers, Mr Abel, see if they can help.'

'Help!?' yelped Abel, gripping his pointing stick as if it were a crossbow. 'There ain't no-one gonna help out here. We're on our own!'

'Except for our five thousand, two hundred and four crewmates . . .' said the Brunt.

As if on cue, at that moment the gyrocopter flew overhead, with the Countess and Mrs Wouldbegood on board. They waved.

'Woo-ooo!' said Rasmussen.

'I'm afraid I can't let you go anywhere! We can't risk giving anything away to these forest drummers. What if they're in league with . . . "You-Know-Who"?' said Abel conspiratorially.

131

'Who's Yoonohoo?' asked Rasmussen.

'He's one of the quartermasters. Lives down on deck three. Plays the fiddle,' said Stanley. 'I'm happy to be in league with him. He's very nice.'

Abel spun round in a tight circle, gripping his stick even harder. He made a noise like an owl, for no apparent reason. Then he turned back to them.

'Not him – I mean . . . Zebediah!'

'Oh, that's okay,' said Rasmussen. 'I'm not sure Zebediah's quite the threat we've always thought him to be. I spoke to someone onboard the FishTank, and they were very keen to tell me that Zebediah isn't really in control any more. It seems the whole thing is falling apart. I told the Captain. He seemed pleased.'

With this bombshell, Rasmussen slurped noisily on her coconut, and threw it over her shoulder. Then she turned away from the Galloon, and pressed through the undergrowth. Stanley and the Brunt followed her, agognised. Abel twitched, and then slipped back into the shadows.

Eyes watched them from every angle.

The pattern of the drums changed.

Cloudier was floating just a few feet above the slightly wonky deck of the Great Galloon, in her little weather balloon. She had become quite adept at piloting the thing nowadays, and now that the Galloon's gigantic main balloon was half deflated, draped at a crazy angle over a rock the size and shape of a cathedral spire, it was possible to fly closer to the deck than she ever had before. It was upsetting to see the Galloon in such a state – although no one had been seriously hurt, the crash had been an almighty one, and the wreckage strewn across the decks would take days if not weeks to clear, repair and reorganise. After the initial shock, the crew and passengers had leapt into impressive action. The Captain was convinced that the Galloon itself was repairable, although it had come to rest at a slight angle, and no-one liked to mention the ominous creaks and groans that came from the hull, especially during the long, hot night they had just spent onboard.

Now, as the work parties were beginning to clear the debris, and save whatever could be saved, it was Cloudier's job to direct them from above, pointing out anything they could not see from the deck itself, such as the hen coops dangling overboard, the crack in the railing just below the poopdeck, and the place where the water barrels had been crushed by a gigantic wooden tiger falling asleep on them. Claude had remained there, as solid and unmoving as the mast itself, since his collapse. Cloudier was concerned about this. She was also concerned about the mainb'loon itself. It was beautiful – the red balloon, the great brown ship smashed against the grey rocks, the green forest stretching out all around. The sky lowered grey and humid, the heat was almost unbearable and the unsettling sound of the drums had not abated, but Cloudier was thankful. She knew, however, that they couldn't stay here forever, and there were many onboard for whom a trek through the forest was unthinkable. So they had to repair her, and repair her they would.

She spotted the Captain, an unfamiliar sight in shirt sleeves and kerchief, leaping from the quarterdeck rail onto the poop. She felt the relief she always felt when he was engaged in the Galloon's business, rather than distracted by thoughts of his lost love, as he had been so much over the last few months. She saw her mother leap after him, and noticed how they held hands to steady each other as they ran along the taffrail towards the main deck.

Yes, he doesn't seem to worry about Isabella so much any more, she thought.

She brought the balloon up, and up, until she was alongside the red canvas of the main balloon still partly pumped up because of the infrastructure that she had seen inside it, and because some of its precious gas must have remained within.

She saw a tiny figure, roped up and harnessed, heaving itself up the side of the balloon near where it was snagged on the rock.

'Clamdigger!' she cried. 'Jack Clamdigger!'

The figure peered over its shoulder and Cloudier was pleased to see it was indeed her friend the cabin boy.

'Clouds!' he cried. 'Can you see where it's caught? Will we get her free, do you think?'

Cloudier raised the little weather balloon a few dozen feet, and peered at the great tear in the fabric, and the shard of rock poking through it. Strands of the mind-boggling floating moss were still escaping from it. It was painful to see, but if she had learned anything from her mother, it was to deal with any situation as it was, not as she would wish it to be. There would be time enough for reflection and poetry later. She returned to Jack's level, and manoeuvred in as close as she dared. He had a huge needle strapped to his back, and a reel of thread over one shoulder. Below him, she could see Tamp, Tarheel, Scrivens and a few other crewmen in a long line, roped together and climbing for all they were worth.

'I think it can be repaired, and if we could refloat her, we could break free of the rock, Jack!' she called. 'And the moss – the floatweed. We could use it, couldn't we? To give us extra buoyancy?' Clamdigger was concentrating once more on climbing, but she knew he heard, as he managed a thumbs up over one shoulder. This was not complacency, she knew – he was focusing hard on the task in hand.

'It's up to me,' said Cloudier, out loud. And she was

pleased with the realisation that this was not some posturing, empty phrase that she had read in a book and liked the sound of. It was the truth.

Between Cloudier and the other flying outriders of the Galloon, they would have to collect enough floating weed from the great spires of rock all around, and repopulate the main b'loon with it. Only then would the Galloon be able to take off, even if they could effect all the necessary repairs, and get the great burners and boilers going again.

She looked around her, and saw the tiny speck of the gyrocopter, away out across the forest. Fishbane had not been with them for many weeks, and Claude seemed to have returned to his unresponsive, wooden state, albeit sprawled across the main deck rather than thrusting out from the bows where a figurehead would normally be seen. Tim and Margery, the crows, should be around somewhere. And that was it.

'Better get on with it, then,' she said to herself. Conscious that she should have girded her loins, but unsure how to, she went about her task.

Out in the forest the drums were yet louder than they had ever been onboard the Galloon. Rasmussen, who was not normally an easy person to spook, seemed spooked. The Brunt, who had taken out a great leather-bound pad and was making notes on likely sources of

dry timber, did not seem too worried. Stanley wasn't sure what to feel. On the one hand, all his experience of unseen drummers in deep forest settings, which was gained entirely from one book called *Danger in the Jungle*, told him that it should be a bad thing. But these drums did not seem malicious to him. Surely if they were a threat, the threat-makers would have made themselves known by now?

'If only we could understand them!' he said out loud.

'Understand what, Stanley?'

'The drums, the Brunt. I have a feeling they are saying something, though not necessarily to us. More . . . about us.'

'About us!' said Rasmussen. 'They better not be talking about me, or I'll give them something to talk about. Which they'd better not!'

'Hmmm,' said the Brunt, as they carried on down the little track they'd been following. 'I once had a friend who spoke drum.'

'A friend who . . . ?' asked Stanley.

'Spoke drum. He would know.'

As he spoke, he pushed through a stand of high grasses, and seemed to stumble out of sight for a moment. Stanley and Rasmussen rushed after him, worried that he had stumbled off an unseen ledge or cliff. But no – he had in fact stumbled out into a clearing. Their eyes adjusted to the distance as they looked out across a wide area of grasses and reeds, where water seemed to have gathered in great waist-high puddles. An elephant, startled at their approach, trumpeted and crashed into the forest a hundred yards away. Birds took off, and monkeys chattered disapprovingly. Even the drums stopped momentarily as if listening, before carrying on their insistent backbeat.

'It's beautiful!' said all three of them together.

From behind a tree at the edge of the clearing, another voice spoke.

'It is, isn't it?' it said. 'The drummers think so too.'

'Who are you?' yelped Stanley, at the bizarrely attired individual who seemed to melt out of the forest.

'Yeah, who are you!?' snapped Rasmussen, incredulously.

'Ah,' said the Brunt. 'Perky Luffington, I presume?'

'At your service, the Brunt, my old sausage!' said Perky Luffington.

GOODNIGHT!

'But, my queen – he is stricken! He will never be weaker! If El Bravado exists, then it will still exist

when we return! But now is the moment to strike at my brother's black heart!'

'You are weak, Zebediah, not he! Once we reach El Bravado, he will be no match for us! With the silver in that lost city, I will be able to buy off his so-called friends, or create an invincible Galloon of my own, or take any one of a million ways to destroy him utterly!'

'You continually underestimate him, my heart, my queen! He is down, but not out. He will be airborne again before you know it – he could yet stop us from reaching El Bravado!'

'Stop bothering me! You are like a gnat, or a flea, nibbling and picking at me till I can take no more. And yet – his tiger is a mighty guardian, I will concur. Perhaps it is best to see to the Galloon once and for all while the wooden beast seems to be recovering.'

'Yes, oh mighty queen. Yes! Shall I give the order?'

'Do not presume so! There is only one here now who is fit to give orders. Hand me the contraption.'

'Here, my lo . . . your highness.'

'SUMBAROONERS. ABOUT FACE. MAKE FOR THE GREAT GALLOON OF MEREDITH ANSTRUTHER. READY ALL WEAPONS!'

Perky Luffington, the Brunt, Stanley and Rasmussen were sitting in the shade of a great spreading tree – not that it gave much relief from the all-pervading heat – while Perky and the Brunt caught up on old times.

'And the time we nearly crashed into the Crystal Tower of PontyCloon, while that Megaduck was trying to eat us! Do you remember?'

'Well, I was deep in the bowels of the Galloon, stoking the furnace. But yes, I heard about it, Perky Luffington . . .' said the Brunt.

'And when the Wampyr of the Gesundheights tried to infiltrate the Galloon, and bit Ms Huntley on the hat! Do you remember that?'

'Well, I was deep in the bowels of the Galloon, stoking the furnace. But yes, I heard about it, Perky Luffington . . .' said the Brunt.

'And when . . .' began Perky Luffington. Stanley felt uncomfortable, and clearly Rasmussen did too, as she jumped in.

'So you grew up on the Galloon, Mr Luffington?' she asked, in full 'daughter of a countess' mode.

'My word no, Ms Rasmussen! I grew up here. I'm Rococan through and through, from the soles of my brogues to the tip of my brolly. I suppose I just . . . took on some foreign ways while I was travelling the world.'

'How fascinating,' said Rasmussen with a smile. 'Then, I wonder if you still notice the drums at all?'

'Drums? Why of course. They're always there, of course, but one notices them. They're a kind of news service, gossip, weather forecast and soundtrack all

141

rolled into one. They've been a bit like a stuck record, of late, though.'

'Oh, and why's that?' asked Stanley.

'Well, they just keep saying variations on the same thing.'

'And what do they say?' asked Rasmussen.

'Let me see . . .' said Perky. 'Well, they seem to be saying Thump-a-Dang-BonkBonk. Thump-a-Dang-CLANKBonk. Thump-a-Dang-BonkBonk. *Pause* Ker-Dang-BonkBonk-DerDUNK!'

Rasmussen and Stanley shared a look – polite, but exasperated.

'And what, pray,' said Rasmussen, in an accent so cut glass it could have actually cut glass. 'What, pray, does that mean?'

'Oh, just a bit of folklore, really. It's so preposterous, it's almost not worth repeating. Must be a slow news day.'

'Tell us anyway, if you don't mind, Perky Luffington,' said the Brunt, who was now leaning forward.

'Very well,' said Perky. 'It means – "Beware the Pirate Queen, scourge of the Great Brown Greasy Rococo. She returns, looking for the lost city of El Bravado. No longer is she alone – she lives in the belly of an iron eel. All will fall before her".'

'Just folklore, you say?' asked Rasmussen, her jaw clenched.

'Oh, now I come to listen, there is a new bit. PurKlank a Klang Kerkonk konk derdonk, on the end.'

'And what does that mean? ' asked Stanley, his mind whirring.

'Oh, I'm so terribly sorry,' said Perky, his brown face paling with fright. 'It says, unless I am much mistaken: "She means to destroy the city-in-the-sky, great cloud-hanger, the whale-of-the-sunrise, floating-canoe-of-the-blustery-realm". I'd thought it was just poetic nonsense, but now I know what made that noise last night, it makes more sense. She means to destroy . . .'

'The Great Galloon!' they shouted as one.

'Meet me back there. I will warn the Captain!' said the Brunt.

To Stanley's astonishment, the Brunt stood up in his thick robe and slippers, and stretched his enormous arms above his head. Then he jumped up and down twice, cracked his huge knuckles, and began to run. Before he had reached the edge of the clearing, he was moving faster than Stanley would have thought possible. As he crashed into the edge of the forest, Stanley realised that he would stop for nothing. Even with the drums and the cacophony of the disturbed birds all around, the noise of the Brunt's progress could be heard for a good few minutes, as he crashed through the under-growth, and no doubt through the overgrowth as well.

'Corks,' said Stanley.

'Well, I guess we should follow,' said Rasmussen. 'Thank you, Mr Luffington.'

'I'm so sorry . . . I didn't put two and two together. The Pirate Queen . . . I thought she was perhaps a myth . . .'

'Perhaps she is. Perhaps she isn't. But without you we would never have known what the drums were saying. So do not apologise. We owe you. Would you care to see the Galloon once more?' said Stanley.

'Yes, dearly,' said Perky. 'And if I can help in any way . . .'

'Of course you can. You already have,' said Rasmussen, as together they set off to follow the trail left by the Brunt's almighty charge.

Cloudier had been working hard. She had found a method of gathering the long, heavy strands of floatweed off the cliff-side, while piloting the weather balloon with one arm. Then she would pile it high in the little balloon, and fly back to the Galloon, where she would stuff it into the tear in the main balloon. Then the sewing party would sew up just enough to keep it in place, while leaving a small gap for the next armfuls. It was hard physical work, and her arms were aching. But every time she returned to the Galloon, she got words of encouragement from the sewing party, which of course included Clamdigger, and that seemed to give her strength.

As she threw her latest bundle of Liken into the balloon, where it fell for a few moments then began to rise under its own buoyancy before becoming stuck under the great red canvas, she looked down. The deck was of course many dozens of feet below. But she could see that progress was being made. Mr Wouldbegood was waving his stick at a group of people who had made a good job of clearing the decks. The Captain and her mother were leading a party of people heaving overboard anything that was giving the Galloon extraneous weight – two grand pianos and a full-size replica of Castle Eisberg had gone over so far, with more to follow no doubt. Cook had set up a kind of soup kitchen on the deck, and all seemed to be progressing smoothly. Despite the apparent difficulty of their situation, the Gallooniers as a team were coping admirably, as ever. Cloudier had no doubt that within a day or two they would be continuing their journey to . . . where? Would they be able to find, let alone follow, the FishTank in this landscape of rocks, water and dense forest?

Never mind, that was a problem for another day. The FishTank would be miles away now, which at least meant that for once they were relatively safe from any kind of attack.

Just as she thought these words, she noticed something extraordinary. Through the forest a few hundred

yards from where the Galloon had come to rest, some-thing huge was moving at great speed. From up here, Cloudier could see the destruction, but she couldn't see what was causing it. Elephants? Great apes? People?

Her heart in her mouth, she began to descend, to warn those on deck in case the thing should turn out to be an enemy. As she sank, she saw that some people onboard had noticed it too. The Captain himself seemed to be the first. With relief she saw that he had stationed lookouts in the forest – crewwoman Neela was hollering from the top of the tallest tree, where she had clearly been set to look for incomers. Cloudier could not hear her, but she heard the Captain's reply.

'The Brunt? Stamp me library books, whoever knew he could move like that!?'

As he said this, he was leaping into the bosun's chair. Without benefit of anybody to wind him down, he simply kicked off the safety latch and plummeted to the ground. At the last moment, he leapt from the little cradle, and landed square on his two feet. Cloudier was now drifting down the side of the Galloon, and she was in a perfect position to watch as the deep, dark undergrowth at the edge of the forest exploded in a flurry of green leaves and smashed branches. Out of it ran something that Cloudier knew could only be the Brunt, though she had never dreamed he could move so fast. He dug two great slippered heels into the ground, and began to slide to a manic halt. Roots and rocks and gouts of mud flew into the air as he ploughed to a halt. The Captain stood firm, until they were standing face to face – or face to belly, at least. As Cloudier touched down nearby, the Brunt leaned his massive hands on the Captain's shoulders and bent down until they were nose to nose. He was panting, but otherwise gave no indication that he had recently been running faster than anyone would have believed possible.

'Hello, Captain Meredith Anstruther,' he said.

'Hello, the Brunt, old pal,' said the Captain. 'Is everything quite well?'

'Yes, Captain,' said the Brunt. 'Except that we may, very soon, be under attack from a Pirate Queen. So the drums say.'

'Ah!' said the Captain. 'Pirate Queen, you say? Well, fear not, old boy. We've been working hard on the old tub, and she should be pretty well able to defend herself against a run of the mill pirate attack. We've seen plenty of those off before, have we not?'

'Yes, Captain,' said the Brunt. 'I hope you're right . . .'

At the same time as the Brunt was arriving at the Galloon, Stanley and Rasmussen were trotting along the wide path of destruction he had created. They were out of breath, and incredibly sweaty. Perky, who was trotting along beside them, seemed unperturbed by the heat, but couldn't stop apologising for his lateness in warning them of the Pirate Queen.

'I don't even know if there IS a Pirate Queen!' he was sobbing. 'Some people say she came through here years ago, threatening everybody and looking for the lost city of El Bravado, but then they also say she gave up, and went off to marry some sailor, or explorer, or something. Turned to the good, they say.'

'I'm sure . . . the Captain . . . will get to . . . the bottom of it . . .' said Stanley, gasping for breath that wouldn't come.

Rasmussen was, if anything, struggling even more than Stanley, because of the Examinator strapped to her back. She stopped for a moment and held her side.

'I've . . . got a stitch . . .' she said. 'Do you think we could leave the Examinator here . . . and get it later . . . ?'

'Yes, of course – or not get it later,' said Stanley, thinking this could be a way to free himself from the tyranny of lessons.

Rasmussen unstrapped the big box from her shoulders, and laid it on the ground. As she did so, she must have knocked the 'on' button. First a crackling noise, then a distinct voice came out of the little mesh speaker.

'Breaker, ten four, big buddy, this is Sidney and Ragnarsson calling the Galloon. Rasmussen, are you there?'

Rasmussen sank to her knees and grabbed the speaktophone.

'Come in, Ragnarsson and Sidney, But please only say normal things, not "breaker" or "ten four", over.'

'Copy that . . . I mean . . . we understand,' said the voice. *'We have to warn you – the FishTank, as you call it, has changed course – we're making straight for the Galloon! They want to wage war on your captain! Over.'*

Stanley, Rasmussen and Perky looked at each other in shock.

'I can't believe it!' said Stanley. 'Just as the Captain might finally get a chance to rescue Isabella, he's going to be busy fighting off this "Pirate Queen", whoever she is.'

'Ah,' said a pedantic little voice on the Examinator, who Stanley thought must be Sidney. *'We can help you there. Your captain will not have to deal with both Isabella and the Pirate Queen.'*

'Oh?' said Rasmussen, testily. 'And why's that?'

'Because,' said Sidney. *'Isabella IS the Pirate Queen.'*

GOODNIGHT!

150

Perky Luffington's return to the Galloon would have been a happy occasion under any other circumstances. Even as it was, he had so many hearty slaps on the back that he felt winded by teatime. But Stanley could see that a terrible weight was on him.

'If I had known . . .' he kept saying. 'If I had all the pieces, I would have moved sky and earth to tell the Captain the truth about this woman, however hard it would be for him . . .'

People consoled him, made him tea, listened to him – but it didn't make it any easier for anybody.

In the end, cowardice had won the day. Stanley and Rasmussen had told the Countess, who had told Ms Huntley, who had, surprisingly, told Abel. Abel and the Captain had retreated to his cabin, the Captain looking drawn and haggard as he knew something terrible was going on.

Stanley and Rasmussen had not hidden in their little eavesdropping hidey-hole. They had waited on deck, with everyone else. There had been no ranting, no smashing of fists on desks. The Captain had simply returned to the deck a short while later, looking tight-lipped but resolute. Abel had his hand on the Captain's shoulder. Stanley thought he had seen a look pass between the Captain and Ms Huntley, but as they were grown-ups and therefore continually giving each other knowing looks of little subtlety, it was hard to tell whether this one meant anything in particular.

'I have led you across the world on a wild goose chase. My only mitigation can be that it was done for the best of reasons – love.'

This was all the Captain said, before climbing the mast to oversee the work that had been done on the balloon.

The FishTank was approaching. Onboard was not only the Captain's brother, who now seemed as feckless as he was evil, but his onetime bride-to-be, the dread Pirate Queen Isabella. Together Stanley, Rasmussen, Cloudier and Clamdigger had painted all of these strange goings-on into one big picture. And yet here they sat in the canteen, great mugs of tea in hands, while the grown-ups around them tried to save the day. The Captain had rallied himself enough to request that anyone who still felt inclined to help him should redouble their efforts at the repairs. Everybody had. Night was drawing in once more, regular as clockwork in this tropical place, and it had been another busy day. The Galloon was in better shape than it had been, but not yet ready to fly. Ms Huntley had commended Cloudier on her peace of mind in restoring the Liken to the mainb'loon. The Captain had persuaded Clamdigger to stop sewing and fixing, climbing and repairing for a few hours, and take some rest. The Countess had told Rasmussen that her sharp thinking with the Examinator may have given them the warning they needed to prepare for the assault. No-one had spoken specifically to Stanley. For the first time since joining the Galloon almost two years before, he was missing his home and his parents. He couldn't even talk to them – the Examinator was still out in the forest, which was now a no-go area. Everybody had been confined to the Galloon, if confined is the right word for such a massive place.

'We don't even know whether the FishTank is any match for the Galloon, in the air or on the ground,' said Cloudier, hopefully.

They all nodded in agreement.

'Though if the Pirate Queen was responsible for transforming the Sumbaroon into such a formidable vessel, then she has surely the capability to make it almost invincible,' said Clamdigger, staring into his cup.

'Thanks for that, Mr Sunshine,' said Rasmussen.

'Sorry,' said Clamdigger. 'But I'm just saying . . .'

'This is the Captain we're talking about!' said Stanley. 'Captain Meredith Anstruther and his Great Galloon! Think of all the scrapes he's got us out of in the past!'

'The volcano,' said Rasmussen.

They nodded.

'Although technically, he got us into that, and Cloudier and the Brunt got us out,' said Stanley.

'There were the Boomaphone noises!' said Clamdigger.

'Yes!' said Cloudier. 'Although that was Rasmussen and Stanley, wasn't it, really?'

'The BeheMoths?' said Clamdigger.

'Cloudier, if you think about it. And you, Jack.'

'What about Fassbinder, the robot spy? The Captain knocked his block off!'

'True! True! Hear hear!' they all muttered.

'But quite a lot of it's been us, hasn't it?' said Cloudier.

'Yup,' said Rasmussen, who'd never experienced a moment of self-doubt in her life.

'So . . . why have we persuaded them to let us sit down here?' said Clamdigger. 'Let's get up on deck and see what's going on!'

'Okay!' said Stanley.

And so they did. As one, they left the canteen, and jumped on the back of Clamdigger's dog-cart. This took them to the for'ard heckscalator. This moving walkway, an innovation of Clamdigger's, took them all the way past the ballroom, the high street and the

Royal Opera House to the upper hatchway, from where they could climb up a spiral ladder to the main deck. They travelled in silence, but as they emerged onto the deck, near the twelve great trunks of the mast, each and every one of them gasped. Stanley felt the blood rush to his ears. In the past few hours, while they had been sleeping, resting and eating, the Galloon had been transformed. It was no longer a shipwreck. It was a fortress.

The main balloon had been inflated once more, and was standing proudly above them. Smoke was billowing from the funnels, so that Stanley knew the Brunt's work of re-stoking the furnaces was well under way. All around the rail, barricades had been built, using spare planking coils of ropes, great nets full of hammocks, furniture and mattresses. Stanley whirled around, and saw that the quarterdeck was now more like a castle turret, built up and thickened with trees from the forest. The harpoon, which Stanley had once seen used to fight off the all-devouring BeheMoths, was now a bunker, surrounded by sandbags, aiming into the forest. Perky Luffington was standing by it, and he tipped his odd hat at them as they emerged. He was surrounded, Stanley now saw, by some people who were new to the Great Galloon. Some were in shorts and sandals, some in strange robes, others in what looked like swimming costumes. Many of them

155

had bow and arrows in their hands, and they all looked ready for a fight.

'My friends, the Rococans!' said Perky, proudly. 'Once the drums put the word out, everybody comes together!'

Stanley felt a lump in his throat, fear in his heart, and a niggling thought in the back of his mind. He walked towards Claude's outstretched finger, the size of a sofa, and touched it – but no, the tiger was still dormant. Perhaps he had had his moment. It looked to Stanley as if he had always been there – indeed some of the planks of the deck seemed to merge into the wooden fingers and claws, as if the tiger had been carved here where he lay.

WHEN THE TIME COMES AGAIN, LITTLE BLUE
Had he imagined it? Perhaps. Perhaps he had imagined it all. He shook his head to dislodge such gloomy thoughts, and turned to see where the others had gone. Rasmussen was sitting, chirpy as ever, atop the great harpoon, looking out to the forest.

Stanley climbed up next to her and peered over the edge of the rampart, at the wide expanse of forest below. The river snaked through it, reflecting the sun into their eyes despite the cloud cover. It was still mercilessly hot.

'Alright, ugly?' said Rasmussen. Stanley knew her jollity was slightly forced – she always got more insulting as she got more tense. 'I know! Perhaps you're a yeti?'

'A blue yeti?' said Stanley.

'Stranger things have happened at sea,' she said.

'Yep. And in the air. We've seen most of them.'

They looked out across the forest.

'What's gonna happen?' she said.

'A fight. Or not. Let's see,' he said.

'We'll see soon,' she said, pointing out across the forest.

Stanley looked, and saw that, where she pointed, something strange was happening to the forest. Along the line of the river, trees were rattling, then shaking, then disappearing with a crash. The trail was moving towards the Galloon, and Stanley knew it could only be the FishTank, making an almost frontal assault.

'Here she comes,' said Stanley. 'I wonder if she knows who she's dealing with?'

'Of course she does – she was engaged to be married to him not long ago!' said Rasmussen.

'You know, on this occasion I didn't just mean him.'

Rasmussen looked at Stanley, and they smiled at each other.

Up the mast, Perky Luffington was emerging from the main balloon, with Cloudier right behind him. Clamdigger had waited in the crow's nest.

'Well, I'm jiggered!' he said. 'You know – I was

onboard for seventeen years, and never knew anything whatever about this. I left the Galloon because I missed the forest, the wildlife, the heat. And all the time we had the forest, the wildlife, and the heat with us. If only I'd known.'

'The Captain needs someone to tend it all, you know – now we've reintroduced the Liken, it may take a long time to re-establish itself. The B'loondeer will need feeding and managing . . .' Cloudier was saying.

'Well, where there's B'loondeer there's always sackrabbits, and where there's sackrabbits there's moon hawks. I bet there's a whole ecosystem in there . . .'

Perky seemed to be in a reverie as he continued. 'I couldn't do it on my own – but I know some of my Rococan friends are desperate for adventure . . . do you think he'd allow it?'

'You know, I think he would?' said Cloudier, with a look at Clamdigger. 'Besides, I think we've earned the right to make some decisions of our own.'

They turned and looked out across the forest, to where the FishTank was blazing its trail of destruction through the trees.

'She's coming!' said Cloudier.

'And him,' said Clamdigger.

'Oh yeah. And him,' said Cloudier.

GOODNIGHT!

A couple of hours later, the FishTank had arrived at the opposite bank of the Great Brown Greasy Rococo River, about a half a mile from the Galloon's rocky resting place. The Gallooniers stood ranged across the top of their makeshift walls, and watched. From where Stanley sat, the FishTank was a long way down and a long way off, but it was still clearly an impressive and formidable machine. Fully half the length of the Galloon, armoured and bristling with spikes and legs and hatches. Many of the crew and passengers of the Galloon had eyeglasses and telescopes. Stanley borrowed one, and watched through it as a long brass tube grew from the front of the FishTank, until it was as high as some of the surrounding trees.

The periscope, he knew. They were watching him watching them.

But it turned out it wasn't just a periscope. A small cone emerged from the end, and this turned out to be a version of the Squeaking Tube, which could project a voice across the intervening space.

'I am going to come out now, Merry,' it said. That was all.

A murmur ran along the serried ranks of Gallooniers. The Captain was on the quarterdeck, where the walls were lowest. Stanley could see him standing with one mighty boot on the rail. He didn't move as the voice of his treacherous love echoed across the valley.

Turning his attention back to the FishTank, Stanley saw a small hatch open behind the periscope. A head popped out and ducked back, then came out again more confidently.

So she's not sure no-one will shoot her, even from here, thought Stanley.

Then there she was. Isabella Croucher, the Captain's fiancée, though Stanley was willing to bet that that arrangement would be broken at the next available opportunity. She looked small, but then she was small, physically. But she had done something no-one else had ever done – brought Captain Meredith Anstruther to his lowest ebb. She seemed to be holding something in her hand – the Squeaking Tube, or whatever equivalent device let her voice ring out, Stanley guessed.

'Hello, Merry,' she said, as if they had met for high tea in the Bitz hotel. 'How lovely to see you again.'

The Captain still said nothing. Behind Isabella, the hatchway was still open, and now another head appeared. Even in this heat, the head was still wearing

161

the great black hat that Stanley still thought of as the Captain's. A shot rang out – a musketeer in the rigging perhaps – and the hat spun round twice before coming to rest again. Zebediah froze.

'Not a bad shot, from that distance,' said Isabella, conversationally. 'But before you shoot again, hear this. The high ground, literally and morally, is yours, Meredith. You can afford to listen. Tell them.'

The Captain's voice, which needed no amplification, thundered out one word.

'Hold.'

'Thank you. So – if you shoot at us again, I will kill Zebediah.'

At this, Zebediah froze, halfway out of the hatch. Stanley realised that he may have been trying to sneak up on Isabella. He was discovered. Isabella spoke on, without looking at him.

'I would have your Galloon, Meredith. No more. It is, you will have guessed, all I wanted. With it, and the riches of El Bravado, I would be invincible.'

Stanley jumped as the Captain's voice crashed across the valley again.

'You could have had it. We would have owned it together.'

'Yes. I thought so too. But you are so . . . good, Meredith. A lifetime on the Galloon would have felt like a hundred, if I had had to keep up that sorry act.

162

We would, no doubt, have spent our time visiting "interesting places" and "making friends" with people. WHERE'S THE FUN IN THAT?'

'I could have shown you the world,' said the Captain.

'I can find the world for MYSELF!!' screamed Isabella, and it seemed to Stanley that here her façade of calm cracked completely.

'Corks,' he said to himself.

'Why should I not kill you? I have the means,' said the Captain.

'Would you be judge, jury and executioner, Captain? Would your people follow you then? A man who would kill them if they stepped out of line?'

'You have done more than step out of line, madam!' cried another voice, and Stanley realised with shock that it was Abel, his voice cracking with emotion.

'Have I? I pretended to be nice, that is all. Don't we all do that, most of the time, Mr Abel? Is it worth a life?'

'I would have given you my life,' said the Captain.

'You yet may,' she snapped back. 'I mean it – I would have your Galloon. You will come to me, and we will discuss terms. If we reach them to my satisfaction, I will give you this rather crude battering ram of a craft, and you will be able to make your escape – albeit a rather slow and earthbound one. I will fly off in your Galloon, with as many of your crew and

163

mine who would relish a life of derring-do among
ne'er-do-wells.'

Nearly everyone, thought Stanley, though he didn't
think anyone would actually follow her.

'I will come,' said the Captain, quietly, for him.

Disapproving shouts rang out across the Galloon.

'No, sir!'

'We will fight for you!'

'Let her have your brother! What's he done for us?'

But only Stanley noticed that while the disapproval
was at its loudest, the Captain was already gone. He
ran along the deck, up the quarterdeck ladders, and
out to the rail. Ms Huntley arrived at the same time
as him, and they both looked down, to where one of
the Captain's many secret passages had let him escape.

'He's gone,' she said.

Stanley tried to follow, but the hatch was now
covered with an iron grille – another one of the
Captain's safety features.

'I'm afraid he still hasn't told me everything there is
to know about this ship,' said Ms Huntley.

'Me neither,' said Stanley, to her slight
consternation.

'There!' cried Jim Braggins. 'The Captain! He's swimming the Rococo!'

Before Stanley could even stop to wonder where Jim
Braggins' accent had gone, he saw that what he said

was true. Somehow the Captain was already off the Galloon – some tunnel or slide had clearly taken him right to the very bottom of the craft and shot him out into the water – and now he was swimming across the river. Here above the falls it was not the great, slow, greasy thing it was lower down. There were rocks and rapids and white water every few feet. Stanley watched the Captain drag himself to his feet to cross a shingle bar, only to throw himself back into the water where it ran deeper. He was being dragged downstream, but he managed to right himself, and after an agonising time, the Gallooniers even managed to cheer as he emerged on the far bank. They saw that Isabella offered him no help at all as he heaved himself up to the side of the FishTank, and then used its scales to clamber upon to the top. Stanley ached to know what was being said over there, but all he could see was a dumb show. To his agognishment, the Captain and his brother embraced. But then Isabella seemed to shove them apart, and stood between them as she appeared to be admonishing Captain Meredith.

It seemed to Stanley that even from here he could hear a few snippets of what the Captain was saying – he wondered whether this was purposeful for the Gallooniers' benefit, or just a by-product of his enormous voice.

'. . . owe those people more than you could ever

know . . . any harm should come . . . if assurances given . . . free to choose, of course . . .'

'He can't be negotiating with her!?' he yelped, like an indignant terrier.

'I think he is,' said Ms Huntley beside him. 'The sentimental old fool.'

'Wha . . . why . . . who . . . ?' said Stanley.

'You see, he thinks he's saving us. He doesn't realise that if he lets her have his way, he will be condemning us, and many more, to a much worse fate . . .'

'That's all well and good,' said Stanley, 'but now he's over there, there's not much we can do except see how things turn out? Is there?'

'Oh Stanley,' said Ms Huntley. 'There is so much we can do. He left me in charge, you see. And my conscience is a much more pragmatic thing than his.'

'What does pragma . . . ?' Stanley began, and then stopped, because Ms Huntley had grabbed a Squeaking Tube, switched it to 'Broadcast', and spoken three words.

'FIRE THE HARPOON!'

Stanley turned to see Rasmussen leap off the harpoon gun in question, fractions of a second before two burly crewmen twisted it round on its great iron stand, aimed it in what Stanley thought could only be a half-hearted way, and then pulled its mighty trigger. A plume of steam emerged from one end, and a lance the length

166

of a rowing boat flew out of the other. The great arrow was usually tied to a rope, so that it could be hauled in again after each shot. But this was clearly a one-shot only operation. Stanley watched as thousands of people leaned in to follow the arrow's path. It seemed as if he had all the time in the world to watch it spin out across the edge of the Galloon and into open space. He flicked his telescope back to his eye, and saw that the three people on top of the FishTank had seen it too. To his amazement Isabella had time to whip out a long curved sword and wave it at the Captain, who ducked. While the arrow still seemed to be crawling across the valley, spinning lazily, Stanley watched as Isabella shoved the Captain bodily with her shoulder. He seemed about to lose his footing. As he leaned out over empty space on his gigantic tippy-toes, she grabbed him by the kerchief around his neck. All this had taken but a moment – the arrow was still only halfway to them. A roar rose from the Gallooniers as the Captain almost fell, and then a hiss as he was saved, but ended up at the mercy of the Pirate Queen. Then there was a kind of confused shrug of a noise as the Gallooniers watched the Captain's brother, who they had always thought of as his mortal enemy, leap at Isabella. She raised her sword with her spare hand, and they heard the Captain's roar.

'NO, Zeb!'

Just at that moment the huge arrow reached them. Isabella swung the Captain round by his kerchief so that he would be in the line of fire, and it seemed to Stanley that Zebediah made a leap to try and get in its way. It took his hat off – the great black thing he had stolen from the Captain all those months ago – and pinned it to the conning tower of the FishTank. Zebediah plunged off the FishTank and into the water.

And that was it.

'Drat,' said Ms Huntley.

'Ha! You got his hat!' yelled Rasmussen triumphantly. 'Oh – that's not enough, is it?'

Isabella grabbed the Squeaking Tube again and spoke.

'A foolish move, Harissa! I know it is now clear that I will not be marrying old Merry here – but if you get him killed, then you won't be able to either!'

'Dunno what she means,' muttered Ms Huntley. Stanley could almost feel the heat of Cloudier's embarrassment, though she was way up in the crow's nest.

'Stop, please!' cried the Captain. 'Everybody, stop risking your lives for me! If we do as she says we can return to our homes, we can carry on our lives. Where's the harm? I accede to your request, Isabella, and will show you how to fly the Galloon.'

'I doubt it!' cried Isabella, and Stanley watched as she used her curved sword to hook something from round the Captain's neck. 'I know how to drive it! I just need the other half of this amulet, this . . . love token . . . to do so. Thank you! Now tell your loyal goons to leave the Galloon within the next hour, no heroics, and no-one will get hurt. You have no idea of the firepower of this craft, and I will destroy the Galloon rather than lose it. Believe me.'

'Do it, my friends. It is the only way,' said the Captain.

'No!' they cried. And, 'Never!'

'Please! Harissa, Birgit? Will you promise me? No more heroics?' called the Captain.

Near Stanley, Ms Huntley said nothing, but her head dropped.

'It seems I have cowed you at last! Perhaps you are not such Able Skymen – and women – after all!'

At this last, Stanley heard another noise. It was like a large kettle finally reaching the boil. Or an air raid siren that has been set to 'annoying squeal'. It wasn't much of a noise, in the great scheme of things. But what it signified was this:

Able Skyman Abel had had enough. Just about blinking well enough.

The Gallooniers around him stood back, and made a little ripple in the wall of bodies. Stanley watched from his vantage point on the quarter deck, and saw that Abel was standing stiff as a board, one arm raised directly above his head, with his little rusty sword held high in it. His face was puce, which Stanley now knew to be a very bright shade of pink. As he watched, he realised that the noise Abel was making wasn't just a noise. It was a word.

'Ssssssssssssffffffffffffffffkkkkkkkkkkksskkkkkkchchch-chchchchchchchchCHCHCHCHCHCHCHCHCHCHCC-CCCCHCHHHHHHHHHAAAAAAAAAAR-RRRRRRRRRRGGGGGGGEEE!!!!!!' he cried.

'Did he say "charge"?' asked Jim Braggins.

'Yes, I believe he did,' replied the butler, Scrivens.

'I thunken no beggar'd ever shout ruddy "charge"!' said Jim. 'Too much flimmin' talking these posh'uns get up to. Now it's time to grarz some flink over the tooting tumpstones, alright!'

'Well, quite,' said Scrivens.

And together, the Gallooniers charged. Stanley even pulled his little sword out of its scabbard, for perhaps the second time ever. The Gallooniers used the coils of rope that formed the barricade itself to fling themselves overboard. They flung the hammock nets to the ground to break their fall. Within a few short minutes, all of them, the entire crew, passengers and all, were in the river, splashing and shouting and heaving themselves across. Stanley saw Clamdigger busily arranging a party to make pontoon bridges out of the debris that had come over with them. Last off the ship was the Brunt, his great dressing gown flapping, his horns glinting magnificently in the sun. He stayed out of the water, as the cold would be deadly to him, but he flung himself across the make-shift bridge at breakneck speed. Stanley was dragged along with the crowd, and was almost across when he looked again at the FishTank. Its crew too were disembarking – pouring out of the conning tower like a fizzy drink overflowing from its bottle. They took up positions on the far bank – they looked to Stanley to be greater in number than he thought, and better armed than the Gallooniers. But even as he rushed towards them, he could see that they didn't have the stomach for a fight. Some of them even turned and half-heartedly faced their own side, as if switching allegiances.

The Captain was now leaning far out over the rapids, still a hundred yards from where the Galloon army was approaching.

'Stop!' yelled Isabella into her Squeaking Tube. 'You think I will not kill him? I will – I am not like you. I can take the Galloon by force, and I do not need him any more.'

The army clattered to an uncertain halt, mostly on the makeshift bridge, some still waist deep in the water.

'In fact,' said Isabella, and now they could see the weird smile on her lovely face as she spoke. 'Why wouldn't I, at this point? You're going to come at me anyway. I don't want him chasing me around, causing trouble, when I'm flying his Galloon around the world, having fun.'

And she dropped him.

It was a fall of some fifty feet, into rocky rapids. The Captain did not scream or yell. He just fell into the water, where he fell limp, and was washed quickly downstream, towards the waterfall. Isabella laughed, and threw his best hat in after him.

'Captain Meredith Anstruther!' cried the Brunt. Everyone else, including the FishTank crew, was silent.

'Attack then!' cried Isabella, for all the world like an irate mother talking to a toddler.

Her crew, many of whom seemed as stunned as the Gallooniers, raised their weapons, and strode out into the shallows. Rasmussen appeared beside Stanley, and for the first time ever, she seemed to have real tears in her eyes.

'We're just children!' she said. 'Why are we here in this battle?'

'Don't tell me you're scared, because you're not . . .' began Stanley, lamely. 'Actually, you are, aren't you? So am I. But what else can we do? Watch from the sidelines?'

And together, they strode into the melee. As they arrived at the front, where the FishTank crew were putting up an unspirited defence, Stanley and Rasmussen found themselves in a tight circle of grown-ups – the Brunt, the Countess, Mr Wouldbegood and Cook, none of whom would let so much as a clip round the ear reach them.

The battle seemed to be going the FishTankers' way anyway, when another cry from Isabella made everybody stop and look.

'Pathetic!' she yelled, from her vantage point on top of the vessel. 'We'd better speed things up, I think!'

She seemed to kick some kind of lever with her foot, and a panel in the side of the FishTank opened up. With a whirring and a hissing, while the crews paused in battle to watch, a great brass mortar cannon emerged. A short fat tube like a barrel, with the mouth carved in the shape of a wolf's maw. Two long mechanical arms placed it on the ground on the riverbank.

'I didn't want to use this against the Galloon, where it could damage my prize,' said Isabella. 'But there's no harm in using it against *people*, is there?'

She lit a long match, and from up on the FishTank she threw it into the mouth of the mortar, which was pointing almost straight up into the air.

'What's gonna . . .' Rasmussen said. Then the world went foom.

Just foom.

Not even particularly loud, though it did seem to block out all other noise. And render the watchers deaf for a spell.

Stanley saw something shoot out of the mortar. Something like a bunch of grapes, only much much bigger and more menacing. It flew up into the air, where

173

it seemed to balance for moment, before breaking apart into many smaller somethings.

'Cannonballs,' he said to Rasmussen beside him.

'No,' she said. She knew a thing or two about cannon-balls. 'Bombs.'

The huge cluster of bombs, of the old-fashioned 'light the fuse and run away' type, had now become a shower of many individual bombs. The FishTank crew seemed genuinely amazed that their Pirate Queen, mad though she had proven herself to be, would think them this expendable. The Gallooniers just knew their time was up.

'Well, Stanley, old bean, it's been good knowing you,' said Perky, affably. 'You know, I really thought the cavalry would arrive.'

'The cavalry?' said Stanley, as the bombs stopped hanging in the air and started falling in earnest.

'Figuratively speaking. It was an experiment of course, but I truly thought that in this global age, the word would get out.'

'What word? What do you mean?' asked Stanley as the bombs brushed the tops of the overhanging trees.

'The drums, lad! Once the drums put the word out, everybody comes together!'

'Wha?' said Stanley, not for the first time.

'SKKwwaaaAAAKKKKakkkaakkkkkkkkkkkkkkkk-aawwwwwwKeraaaaQuawwwkaaakkaaaaaaaAAA!' said somebody overhead.

Stanley stood, agognished once more. Above him, Fishbane, the lord of the Seagles, had appeared. He seemed to have sprung fully formed from thin air, though it was much more likely he had simply been out of view above the trees.

'SquueeeeeeeeKallakkkalakkkalakka-KahoooooooooooooooooeeeeKKK!' said a different voice, and Stanley whirled around to see another Seagle, and another, and another.

'Fishbane!' he yelled.

But Fishbane was busy. He had grabbed one of the bombs in his sharp, webbed claws. Each of his many companions had also grabbed one each. With another screech, he seemed to direct his cohorts towards the FishTank, where Isabella was now dancing, wild with rage and fear.

'Nooo!' she screamed. 'Drop them, you thieving birds!'

And so they did. Each Seagle dropped its load of bombs down the open chute of the FishTank's conning tower. About thirty bombs must have gone down there in not nearly as many seconds. Many of the Seagles added a little extra payload of poop too, as a mark of disrespect. With a final swoop, Fishbane knocked the hatchway shut with his great beak. The crew members of both vessels whooped and cheered, Stanley noticed. Within seconds, the FishTank began to leap and bounce like a cracker as the bombs went off within. Huge lumps and dints appeared in its pristine outer surface, and soon it was looking as battered and bedraggled as the Sumbaroon ever had. It lay, motionless, in the shallows. With one final boom, the conning tower flew open and a burst of poopy smoke flew out. There was another cheer from the crowd. Isabella had been clinging on for dear life, but when she saw that the explosions had finished, she stood up again.

'Fools! I need it not, this stopgap machine! I am to be the Pirate Queen of the Great Galloon, do you not see? And where is your Captain to save you now?'

Her words struck Stanley to the core once more – the Seagles had destroyed the FishTank, but they could not bring the Captain back.

OH YES THEY CAN

Well, this was strange. He hadn't thought that thought, had he?

NO SMALL BLUE

Small blue. Who calls me small blue? thought Stanley.

CLAUDE CALLS YOU SMALL BLUE

'Claude!' said Stanley out loud. 'Of course! But he's . . .'

Around Stanley, people were standing in the river, on the bank, on the bridge, all unsure of where to look next. Isabella seemed to be trying to free some new contraption from a mooring point on the FishTank's back. A backpack? A vacuum cleaner?

HE'S BEHIND YOU

Stanley whirled around.

AND THE WORD YOU'RE LOOKING FOR IS JETPACK

Never mind agognished, Stanley was bemazed, astonified and besidehimselfinated by what he saw. There was Claude, magnificent as ever, flying low over the river. In one great rear claw he held the Captain, who waved a great hand and beamed at them all. In the other was Zebediah, who seemed to be out for the count. Around them was a veritable fleet, a squadron, a flotilla of flying machines of all shapes and sizes.

'Charlie!' cried Stanley, as he recognised a young lad who had been given a second chance by the Captain not too long ago.

'There's the Count!' yelped Rasmussen, as a gyro-copter slightly swankier than the Galloon's hove into view.

'Little Ern!' cried the Sultana of Magrabor, and soon many voices were joining in, as they recognised friends and relations.

'Mum! Dad!' cried Stanley at last, as his parents chugged into view on a spindly, pedal-powered thing, his father riding pillion while his mother steered.

'Stanley, my wonderful boy!' cried his father, as they landed on the bank – the FishTankers seemed to be either joining in, giving up or running for the hills.

'So this is what you get up to!' shouted his mother over the melee. 'Well, it seems like fun – perhaps we should stick around!'

Stanley grinned and began to wade towards them. Rasmussen caught up with him and they waded together.

'And is this your little girlfriend?' asked his mother, on seeing Rasmussen.

'MMMuuuuu—uuuuuuuuuummmmm!' whined Stanley.

'Don't make me laugh, Mrs Crumplehorn,' said Rasmussen. 'I can do better than him!'

GOODNIGHT!

Cloudier was disappointed to hear that Isabella had got away. She slipped down from the FishTank during the celebrations at the Captain's return, and disappeared into the forest. Some said he had asked that no-one follow her. Some said he had been too busy kissing Ms Huntley to notice, though Cloudier didn't like to think about that.

Refloating the Galloon, though still a mighty undertaking, had been a lot easier with so many flying companions and contraptions to assist. Claude heaved from below, the Seagles pulled at the mainb'loon, and the various planes and copters helped keep her steady, provide extra lift, and a hundred other useful things. The Brunt had been suffering from mild hypothermia after the battle-that-never-was, but once they had flown him back onboard and he had regained his little room, he was feeling fine and stoking furnaces again in no time.

A few days after the refloating, once Claude had said his goodbyes and retaken his place at the prow, and the Galloon was heading downriver towards the open sea, Stanley and Rasmussen were sitting on some coils of rope on the maindeck, watching the sun either go down or come up. With them were a fierce-looking girl in a peach-coloured ball dress, and a small boy who appeared to have a pair of scaly wings sprouting from his back. Sidney and Ragnarsson, who had been such a help from inside the Sumbaroon. Stanley and Rasmussen had been showing them around the Galloon, teaching them the real rules of backgammon, and generally making them welcome.

'You'll like it here,' said Stanley. 'It's very quiet – not a lot going on, if you know what I mean. But we're sure that something's gonna kick off soon, aren't we, Rasmussen?'

'Oh yeah,' said Rasmussen. 'It's high time there was an adventure of some sort round here.'

'Oh no,' said Ragnarsson. 'We don't like adventure, do we, Sidney Dragonback?'

'Nope,' said Sidney, munching a teacake. 'Anything for a quiet life, that's our motto.'

Stanley and Rasmussen exchanged awkward looks, and moved slightly further away from the newcomers.

'Captain Anstruther and Ms Huntley getting married, eh? Tsk,' said Rasmussen.

'I know! Where did *that* come from?' said Stanley. They both rolled their eyes at the capriciousness of grown-ups.

'So – do you think we'll ever get this adventure we've been waiting for?' asked Rasmussen.

'You know what?' said Stanley. 'I'm not sure. Perhaps it's okay for us to live a quiet life for a little while.'

'BOOOOOORRRRRRIIIINNNNGGGGGG!!!!!' said Rasmussen.

'Ha!' said Stanley. 'Nearly had you though, didn't I? I hear there's a room near the prow that's got a magic cupboard in it – you go in as you and come out as a cupcake!'

'Mmmmmm,' said Rasmussen. 'I love cupcakes. Let's go and check it out.'

'Okay!' said Stanley.

'Tomorrow,' they said together.

In the crow's nest, Tim turned to Margery.

'What a palaver, eh?' he said.

'Blimey,' said Margery. 'A talking crow!'